may 202=
For Berth
I hope you enjoy ❦

Irene

901. 233.0788
Irene

I

CONTENTS

POSTCARDS
FROM MOM

Hi from Nassau! Our ship docked early this morning and everyone wanted to hurry and eat breakfast, then go gawking and shopping. It's a pretty little town and I already bought you a souvenir. We'll only be here one day, then on to Turks and Caicos. Bye for now!

Hi from Cockburn Town (the name makes me giggle - I'm awful). According to our brochure, the Turks & Caicos Islands are named after the Turk's Cap cactus and a native word "cay" meaning string of islands, isn't that interesting? It's a British protectorate or something. Very pretty, nice shops, but also jungles & swamps. Sounds like Miami, doesn't it, haha! I found the perfect souvenir for you. Dad says it's time for lunch, bye!

Hi from San Juan. Things aren't back to normal yet in PR. Some still have no electricity. Thank goodness we have a/c in our cabin on the ship as it's very hot and humid. But we had some good fish for lunch (don't ask me what kind - I don't remember), and I found a souvenir shop that was open. Bye for now!

❖ ❖ ❖

Hi from Santo Domingo! Historic Spanish bldgs from the 1500s, cobblestone streets, flowers everywhere & nice people.Your dad's been practicing his Spanish with the shopkeepers which slows us down since they speak English better than he speaks Spanish. But I did manage to pick up a few things. Time to get back to the ship. We're on the first shift for dinner. Bye.

Greetings from Oranjestad, Aruba! That's Dutch for Orange City. We docked at night, so since we had all day we decided to take a bus tour. Did you know there's a US-based medical school here called Xavier Univ. School of Medicine? It's a 2-yr pre-med and a 4-yr medical program leading to an MD degree. Classes are taught in English. Maybe you could get a scholarship since your grandparents are Dutch. Just a thought. Duty-free port. Bye!

◆ ◆ ◆

Finally in Roatan, Honduras. Big tourist town. We spent 2 days at sea getting here but it was nice staying on the boat & relaxing. Lots to do here: island tour, visit to iguana farm, scootering around, butterfly garden, cameo factory & many ocean-based activities. You could spend a long time here & lots of $. We ate lunch on board the ship to watch our cash. Your dad took photos of windsurfers. He said if he was 30 yrs younger he'd do it. Sure. Out of room - love you!

◆ ◆ ◆

Hola from Mexico! Actually from the boat. They docked to pick up some food, then we're leaving again, diverting to Key West. From what we're told, 2 drug cartels are shooting the place up. Too bad, we wanted to take the tours of Cancun, Cozumel & Chichen Itza. But it's not safe. I'll have to read up on Key West now. There's a carved ice contest this afternoon & an art sale in the lounge. Maybe I'll score a Picasso among the starving artists, haha! Love you!

◆ ◆ ◆

Back in the States! Key West is great, and everyone speaks English! But there are some very INTERESTING characters here, stuck in the 70s it appears. We took the conch tour this morning and saw old houses, the cemetery, and drove right past the nude beach! It was fun & the driver let us out at all the shops, so of course I went a little crazy. Bought you some sandals from Kinos - hope they fit. Can't return them now, so I'll keep them if they don't. Love you!

◆ ◆ ◆

Hi! We're an hour outside Cape Canaveral where we disembark. I know I didn't have to send a postcard because we'll see you before you get this. We ran around this morning tipping everybody & packing everything. Dad's peeved because between all the souvenirs & duty-free shop purchases the past 13 days, he had to buy 2 more suitcases to put everything in. Hope they fit in the car haha! Can you read my handwriting? Sorry it's getting tiny. We'll be home Sat. & plan to sleep 12 hrs LOL. Dad took lots of photos so you can come over to see the slide show. See you soon, Mom.

◆ ◆ ◆

A DAY IN THE LIFE
OF A DETECTIVE

Morning broke late in the City. The tall edifices of Manhattan created long shadows, and the sun was slow to rise, especially on this cold and windy day in mid-October. I picked up my battered Timex - it was almost eleven. Although it was late in the morning, I reminded myself I hadn't gotten to bed until after three.

I rubbed my eyes, shuffled to the bathroom and turned on the hot water tap, knowing it would take a few minutes to reach my fourth-floor apartment. In the meantime, I picked up the clothes I'd carelessly dropped on the floor and threw them over a chair. Not surprisingly, they smelled of cigarettes and beer; I'd have to take them to the cleaner soon.

Finally, the water was running warm so I filled the sink, and washed my face, digging at the dried crust on my eyelashes with my fingers. A peek in the mirror of the medicine cabinet reflected two red-rimmed eyes with dark bags underneath. Too many two-bit cases, too much beer and cigarettes, too little sleep.

Finishing in the bathroom, I took three steps into the so-called kitchen of my one-room apartment. "Efficiency" they called it when I rented it six years ago. I like it only because I can always sleep with my back to the wall, a plus in my line of business. My sister, Matilda, had brought over a dozen eggs, butter and bread yesterday, bless her. She was worried about me. Heck, I was worried about me, too. I broke a couple of eggs into a buttered pan and cut off a chunk of bread.

Waiting for the eggs to cook, I lit a cigarette and inhaled deeply. The warmth flooded down my throat like good brandy, which I vaguely remembered. Brandy was rare unless someone else was buying, but at fifteen cents, I could afford a pack of Chesterfields.

After breakfast I cleaned up, shaved, dressed, and pulled out my notebook. Last night I had trailed a guy supposedly cheating on his wife. He was cheating all right - at the poker table. I kept an eye on him until he went home. He was up only three bucks minus about seven beers, and she'd probably light into him for that, so I decided not to intrude. I'd drop by later when he was at work, tell her the truth, and get the twenty-five bucks she owed me.

But there was another entry in my notebook, something more potentially lucrative. A wealthy Manhattan matron had let her fingers do the walking and chose my name from the Yellow Pages because she thought it sounded noble. Not the image I was going for, but I didn't say anything. She wanted me to find her poodle - the pedigreed pup was worth two grand. She said she'd pay well (her words) for his return. I told her I don't usually do this kind of thing, so she changed the adjective to "handsomely". Anything to get dear little doggy back again. I decided to head over to her place and had just donned my fedora when the phone rang.

"Sebastian Knight," I answered.

"Oh, Mr. Knight," purred the definitely feminine voice on the other end of the line. "This is Foxy

Troublefield, remember me? We met last night at the Rikki-Tikki Club. You gave me your card and said I should call if I ever needed help."

The name Foxy Troublefield didn't ring a bell with me, but I had rubbed elbows and maybe shoulders with a good-looking gal last night. Petite, dark hair cut in a bob, big round eyes and very nice legs.

"You drank a martini," I said, guessing this was the gal. "Vodka and dry vermouth, and you asked the bartender for an extra olive." There was a sharp gasp on the phone.

"Why, Mr. Knight, you WERE paying attention," she purred happily. There was a slight pause. "I do have a little problem. A silly little problem actually, and I wonder if you could help me out."

I took a moment and stuck a cigarette into my mouth but didn't light up. Psychologically, I figured my words might come out more manly if I had to clamp my teeth together a little. "Sure," I said, "but I have another client right now. Can this wait until the afternoon?" I was hoping I'd find the dog pretty quick.

"Yes, of course. In fact, closer to dinnertime would be better. How does six o'clock sound?"

"Sounds fine," I answered. Give me your address and phone number." I wrote down the information on my notepad wondering what her angle was. Meeting for dinner at her house didn't sound like a difficult case.

"See you later," I said and hung up the phone, then lit my cigarette. It sounded interesting, very interesting. But first I had to see a dame about a poodle.

The address I'd gotten from the poodle's owner was on Madison at East 79th Street, a couple of streets from Central

Park and the Metropolitan Art Museum. Very, very fancy with a doorman. Long story short, the lady was beside herself with worry. She was afraid her sweet boy, "Coiffure Haute Maintenance Jacques" (or Jack, for short) had been dognapped. I asked for a photo and she provided me with plenty, taken in Central Park, from every angle.

I left the sobbing woman to her butler and maid, then took the subway to the Humane Society and showed them the multitude of pictures. Within ten minutes, High Maintenance Hairdo Jack was on a leash (I'd have to charge her for that since it was extra) and we were walking down the street. I have to give it to this foo-foo boy; he was perfect on the leash and thoroughly enjoying this excursion outside his luxury penthouse, walking with a distinct spring in his step. I think he must have marked two dozen trees. We killed two hours in Central Park, then walked two blocks to the penthouse. He gave me a look that could only mean, "Thanks, buddy, that was the best time I've had in years!" I petted him on the head, gave him a wink, collected my money, pulled my fedora over one eye, and whistled while walking to the subway.

It was almost four o'clock, so I had a couple of hours before going to Miss Troublefield's apartment for dinner. After all that exercise with Jack, I needed to clean up and shave again. This time I tried a little Brilliantine to shine up my hair which I wore in the style of Gary Cooper, parted on the left. My mirror approved.

At six o'clock on the dot I was at her entryway. I rang the bell for her apartment and the familiar voice cooed, "I'm buzzing you in, Mr. Knight. I'm in 2-D."

When she opened the door, I noted her apartment was bigger than mine, but then everybody's was. There was a bedroom on the right and a little sunroom off the kitchen. But I was stymied. I was here for dinner and didn't smell anything cooking. I got suspicious. "Was I supposed to bring dinner?" I asked, turning to face her full-on. It was a nice face.

"Oh, no, Mr. Knight!" she exclaimed. "But to be truthful, I'm not much of a cook."

"So…?" I asked, hoping she'd fill in the rest.

"When you gave me your card last night, Mr. Knight, you said to call if I needed anything. *Anything.* Well, I need help learning how to make a meal. As I said, I'm not much of a cook, but I need to make a meal for a nice man I met. Will you help me out, please?"

Well, what could I say? After looking into those big, round, pleading eyes, I said, "Sure, Miss Troublefield, I'll do the best I can." My mom had been a good cook and I hoped I could remember at least something. "What do you have to work with?"

"Oh, I have pots, pans, utensils, dishes, and all those things," she smiled. "And please call me Foxy. Miss Troublefield sounds so formal." She paused. "May I call you Sebastian?"

"Sure," I answered, starting to feel a little sweat running under my shining hair. "But getting back to dinner, what do you have in the way of food to work with?"

"Oh," she said looking in the refrigerator while I admired the view from behind. "I have a few mushrooms, half a green pepper, two rashers of bacon, half a jar of black olives, a little cheese, a dab of butter, oh, and four eggs. That's not much. Should we run to the store?"

I thought for just a second. "Not necessary, Miss, uh, Foxy. I can show you how to whip up a nice Western Omelet."

Foxy clapped her hands gently and laughed out loud.

"I knew you could help me out, Sebastian! I thought last night you had the look of a fast-thinking man, a man who could come through in a pinch."

"Well, I hope this nice man you met appreciates how you went to all this trouble to impress him," I said, surprised at what I was feeling. I thought this kid was great, and beautiful to boot.

Foxy put a hand on my arm. "I think he does, Sebastian," she whispered. "I like a nice omelet once in a while, but I prefer my private detectives hard-boiled."

Yessir, this had been a very good day, and was about to get better.

MARY, MARY

Well, there I sat sucking on a green Jolly Rancher candy, my favorite flavor, when I sees Ernie ride up on his bicycle. *That bike's seen better days*, I says to myself. When I see Ernie, I think, *So's Ernie.*

"Hey, Ernie, what happened to you?" I asks.

Ernie puts his feet down to stop the bike as the brakes is worn out, like the soles of his shoes, too, but never mind that. "I got in the middle of Big Mary Wilkes and Mary Elizabeth Tooley, to break up a fight," he says, shrugging his shoulders. "I got the worst of it, though. Shoulda let them slug it out. Never try to help the weaker sex, Jonesy, when they gotta get it outta their system."

"Well," says I, nodding my head in agreement and popping another candy in my mouth, "go home and put a steak on your eye."

"Steak?" Ernie laughs. "We got no steak. Ma may have some liver, though. It's leftovers from last night. I can't put it in my stomach, but maybe it'll work on my eye."

Ernie bikes away and I hear yelling. Two angry voices getting closer and closer. Then I hear some words.

"... never been born!"

"... big as a house!"

"... well, I oughta!"

"... Jonesy!"

Uh, oh, one of them says my name. Nervously, I pop

another Jolly Rancher in my mouth because all of a sudden it's dry as a desert.

Around the corner they come, marching towards my stoop. Big Mary Wilkes has her hands made into a fist. Mary Elizabeth Tooley's face is red and scowling. Not good signs. I wonder what I done - or didn't do - to make them charge me like a couple of female bulls.

"How do, ladies," I says with a kind of smile on my face, the best I can do in the circumstances. "What brings you here this morning?"

Big Mary puts her fists on her wide hips. The sun is making her a very large and menacing shadow on the sidewalk. "You know what brings us, Jonesy," she says to me, squinting her eyes.

"Yeah," chimes in Mary Elizabeth.

I think to myself, first of all, for them being named Mary, they sure ain't acting like their namesake. And then I think back quickly on the events of the past week when I was talking to them, but for the life of me, I can't think of anything bad I might of said or done.

Slowly I shake my head from side to side, chewing my bottom lip. "No," I says. "But you may as well tell me what's up because I can't think of one thing."

Mary Elizabeth takes a step forward and I lean back a bit. I don't want a black eye like Ernie's either.

"The dance!" she practically hollers. "The school dance!" she says again like I'm supposed to know what that means. And then a lightbulb brightens up in my brain.

"The spring dance?" I say. "Next Saturday night? What about it?"

"Who did you ask to go?" Mary Elizabeth says.

I spread my hands. "Nobody. I'm not going." I figure that's that, as clear an answer as I can give.

"You didn't ask Mary Joseph Lark?" says Big Mary.

"Or Mary Louise McKenzie?" says Mary Elizabeth.

I shake my head again, saying nothing. But I ponder why all the girls I know are named Mary. Catholics have no imagination, I guess. My own sister's name is Mary Frances.

There is silence, then I ask, "Why did you hit Ernie in the eye? He's at home rubbing liver on it right now."

The girls look at each other, then Mary Elizabeth says, "We saw Ernie riding by and we asked if he was going to the dance next Saturday and he said no. Then we asked if you was going to the dance and he said he thought you asked Mary Joseph or Mary Louise, he couldn't remember which." She looked at Big Mary.

"And we knew you all the way from first grade," continues Big Mary as if that means something special to me. "So we smacked him."

"Why'd you smack Ernie? He didn't do nothing."

"You weren't there," explains Mary Elizabeth.

I nod my head with understanding, but with a little fear, too. "You going to slug me?" I says.

Big Mary sighs. "No, I'm not slugging anybody else today. I don't want to ask forgiveness for two bad things I did today."

"Me too," agrees Mary Elizabeth.

"Okay, then," I says with relief.

We all look at each other and everybody gets embarrassed.

"You sure you're not going to the dance?" Big Mary says, wishing I'd say otherwise.

"No, I don't know how to dance," I admit. "My sister tried to teach me last year, but she gave up. She says I haven't got the right feet."

"You have two left feet," says Big Mary, nodding

wisely.

"I'm pretty sure I don't," I says, looking down.

"No, you say two left feet," she says.

"Right, left, it's all the same," I says. Then I says, "Ernie deserved that shiner for telling a lie."

The girls brighten up and look at each other.

"That's right!" says Mary Elizabeth. "He deserved it."

"He'll rot in Hell," says Big Mary with a little quiver in her voice.

I feel sorry for Ernie. I don't know where he got the notion I was going, but you can't really blame him. After all, there are so many Marys in the neighborhood you can't keep one straight from another, hardly.

Right then my sister, Mary Frances, comes out onto the stoop. "Ma says it's time for lunch." She looks at the other two Marys and waves to them, then says, "Then we have to go with her to the tailor's."

I snap my head around. "What for? I says.

"You don't remember what she said this morning, I guess. You was probably reading the comics at the time. She's taking us to the tailor's today to get her fancy dress cut down for me, and Pa's old suit cut down for you."

Again I says, "What for?"

My sister slaps me in the back of the head and says, "Because you're taking me to the dance Saturday. Don't you remember breakfast last Wednesday? You're taking me because Pa doesn't trust the boys I like at St. Bernard's because they all smoke. Do you remember now?"

I'm rubbing the back of my head where she slapped me, vaguely remembering this conversation in between Little Orphan Annie and Dick Tracy's adventures. Maybe I told Ernie then forgot about it again. But it was still his fault he got all the Marys mixed up.

Big Mary and Mary Elizabeth back up a few steps, then say, "Well, goodbye," and walk away.

I stand up to go inside. As I'm opening the door I hear Mary Frances say, "And when we get back from the tailor's, Ma and I are going to teach you to dance."

I roll my eyes. Heaven help me, Mother Mary!

THE NEW HEART

How can I explain what I'm about to tell you except that I now know that the essence of human nature comes from within and not without. Whether or not you believe me, it's the truth.

My name is Henry Gottlieb. I am a thirty-four-year-old man, the only child of Oscar and Lena Gottlieb, first generation immigrants from Poland. I was educated at the New York Institute of Fashion, and for the past eleven years have been working with my mother's cousin, Irving Ross, on West 38th Street, New York City's Fabric Center. Irving's business is the manufacture and sale of high-end fabrics; I came on as a designer. We have been very successful for a number of years.

So why was I sitting in jail with an appointed lawyer, trying to figure out what put me there? Truthfully, I don't understand it all, but I will tell you what happened.

Chaim Rubin was the attorney assigned to me. He and I were seated in a small cement-lined room with a table between us.

"Now that we have met each other, Mr. Gottlieb," the lawyer said, "I want you to tell me about yourself. It will help me get a better understanding of your background and some insight as to your character."

I looked into his eyes. They were light blue and almost kind. I felt I stood a good chance of going home if

21

this was my attorney. "Then I will tell you my story, every word of which can be corroborated by my parents and associates."

He nodded and I began. "I was born at home; my mother was attended to by a midwife. My parents are from the old country and that was the way things were done. I was a small baby, only a bit over six pounds, so the midwife advised my parents to take me to a pediatrician for a check-up soon. Otherwise, she felt I was healthy. But my parents didn't take me to a doctor. I suppose babies born today are checked right away, but that wasn't the case with me. At the age of two, I developed a fever which resulted in my first visit to a clinic. Besides the fever, it was discovered that my heart was underdeveloped. My mother became hysterical, according to my father, blaming it on herself. She immediately became the essence of a smothering mother; I was not to play with other children or become overtaxed in any way for fear my heart would give out. You can guess what my life was like for the next sixteen years.

"Thankfully, I discovered I had a talent for drawing. I spent my free time sketching, coloring, and painting, even into the evening hours after homework was completed. On weekends when the weather was nice, I liked to sit on a park bench and sketch people going by, especially the ladies in fancy clothes and hats. With an eye for color and style, I realized early on that I should pursue a career in fashion design, so when I graduated from high school, I enrolled at the Institute of Fashion. For the past eleven years, I've been working as a fashion designer on West 38th Street.

"In the meantime, my health was once again declining. My heart hadn't grown much more after I reached my full adult size, so I was always tired and breathless. Sometimes my fingers and toes would turn blue, especially during the winter. Having been under a cardiologist's care for a number of years by then, I agreed to allow him to put me on the list for a heart transplant, as my heart would soon give out. At thirty-two years of age, I wasn't ready to die, so I signed the paperwork. I knew there was a chance no suitable heart would be found, as there were hundreds of other people on the list. But there was no other option for me.

"One morning, almost two years ago, as I was preparing to go to work, I received a phone call from someone at New York-Presbyterian Transplant Institute saying a donor had been found in New Jersey. The heart was being transported at that moment by helicopter, and I was to get to their facility as quickly as possible for surgery. An organ can only remain viable outside the body for about twelve hours, and there was considerable preparation time prior to surgery. After agreeing to get there as soon as possible, I called my parents and Uncle Irving, my employer, to tell them what was happening, then called a taxi to take me to the hospital.

"I was keenly aware of being the center of attention, although I had little knowledge of what was going on in the background. Of course, I knew nothing about the donor except it was a male. I sent him my thanks in a silent prayer and, before too long, I was put under.

"It took hours to awaken from the anesthesia, and I was almost sorry that it was so soon. I felt as if I'd been run over by a car. My eyes couldn't focus for too long, and every time I closed them, I fell asleep for a few minutes. There was much concern, I could tell, because I wasn't responding in a typical way. A realist since childhood, I knew I might not live a long life but was happy to at least have the chance.

"I'll spare you the details of the time I spent in the hospital and consequently in a rehabilitation center. Lucky to have no signs of rejection or infection, I was back home in six weeks. Of course, my parents doted on me, but otherwise everything was as normal as could be expected. I had a model recuperation; within two months I was back at work designing beautiful clothing for beautiful people.

"A year and a half went by with excellent results. I no longer had chest pain and could walk and move about without gasping for breath. I even began dating a lovely model by the name of Rose, who was as beautiful inside as she was outside. She kept an eye on me, making sure I didn't miss my medications, and that I ate healthy meals; even my parents thought she was wonderful. Life was good.

"For the past two weeks we've been working harder than usual as there is another big show coming up Saturday. My designs, if I may be so bold, are stunning and cutting edge, and I wanted Rose to wear the final runway piece. It's beyond description; all I can say is she is breathtaking in the gown. All I wanted to do at the last minute was to add a flowing scarf to fill out the silhouette and accentuate the color of her eyes."

I stopped the narration and looked at my attorney. To his credit, he hadn't fallen asleep. I realized I'd been talking for at least ten minutes without stopping, and he hadn't said a word. His eyes were riveted on me as if he sensed the end of my story was forthcoming.

"And then?" he prompted. I took a long and deep breath.

"Last night Rose stayed a little later than everyone else because we were going to have a late dinner after work. We were both exhausted, and I had to give her credit for

POSTCARDS FROM MOM AND OTHER SHORT STORIES

hanging in there. People think being a model is easy but let me assure you, it's not. Anyway, I decided to whip up that scarf for her, and in five minutes I had it in my hand. It was beautiful, perfectly colored for her complexion, hair and eyes. I draped it around her neck, trying it this way and that, standing back to see the effect.

"And then I heard a voice - a man's voice - saying, 'Make it tighter.'

"I froze in place, unable to move on my own accord.

"It must be tighter ... tighter!"

"And then I saw my hands criss-cross the scarf around Rose's neck, then pull hard. She fought me. Well, it wasn't me, Henry, but some part of me. She was kicking and gasping, yet I couldn't control my actions.

"Rose's eyes began to roll back and I feared the worst. Thank God at that moment Irving walked in because he'd left his cell phone on his desk. When he saw what was happening, he grabbed me from behind and shook me very hard, screaming in my ear to stop, until I dropped the ends of the scarf. Rose fell to her knees. I remained frozen in place while he made sure she was all right.

"While I remained in a catatonic state, Irving called 911 and I was arrested for assault and attempted murder. I tried to tell the policemen that it wasn't me, it was somebody else strangling Rose, but they weren't interested in hearing my story. They told me to be quiet and tell it to my attorney. So here you are."

Chaim Rubin said nothing for a long moment, only drumming his fingertips on the table. "Could it be," he asked slowly, "that your new heart is to blame?"

I stared at him, mouth open. "That's crazy," I answered. "How could that be?"

"Before I came here, I requested a court order to learn

the name of the organ donor, and contacted his parents. I learned he had been a problem child - their words, not mine - and was always getting into scrapes in school. He joined a nefarious motorcycle gang as a young man and had been jailed a few times for assault and felony theft, so he had a record. The day he died, he'd gotten into an argument with his girlfriend and tried to strangle her. She got away and called the police. When he flipped his motorcycle in a high speed chase, it landed on top of him; he was pronounced brain dead at the scene. His parents decided that he should do at least one good thing in his life, and they donated his organs to needy recipients. You got his heart."

I stared at him. "Are you serious? What are you insinuating - that I heard his voice telling me to kill Rose? That's what I have to live with for however long I live? If it is, how can I change my heart? It's not like buying new batteries when the old ones wear out!" My mind frantically bounced from thought to thought, filling me with terror. "Will I kill someone someday?" I asked.

"Honestly, Henry, this is as strange to me as it is to you," Rubin answered. "I'm not sure exactly how I'm going to defend you in court yet, but rest assured, I'll consult as many experts as possible. You can't be the only organ recipient who has been affected in this way. I'll get my team on it immediately." He looked deeply into my eyes. "For the record, I believe Henry Gottlieb is not guilty."

I said nothing and didn't see him leave the room because my eyes were streaming with tears. The guard took me back to my cell to leave me alone with my thoughts. Thankfully, Rose would be fine, but my career was certainly over. How could I exorcise the demon that lived in my heart? Surely, it would happen again, and I would be punished for someone else's actions. What would my future be? My parents would be devastated.

At my arraignment, I told the judge that Henry Gottlieb did not try to kill Rose, and he believed me.

Today I heard the voice say, "Find a rope." Luckily for me, I suppose, I'm not even allowed to wear a belt to hold up my pants in this hospital.

DESCENDING

I have decided I will not go back to see Dr. Charles. He thinks I'm stupid all of a sudden, talking to me in the simplest of terms. I know what a TIA is, I know the difference between that and a full-blown stroke. I know the difference between dementia and Alzheimer's Disease. I realize some medications affect your memory. I know, I know, I know!

Dennis or Joseph always accompany me to see Dr. Charles because I don't drive anymore. Dennis took my keys away last year when I ran over my hibiscus bush and did some damage to the car, not to mention the bush. I told him the sun was in my eyes - it was setting in the west right behind the house after all - and I missed the driveway. But Dennis said it wasn't the first time I'd hit something, so before I ran over something more important than a hibiscus while backing out of the driveway, he took my car keys and promised either he or Joseph would take me to my appointments or shopping. I was so humiliated that I didn't speak to him for a month.

I'm a healthy older woman. Every physical I've had for years has been phenomenally positive. Dr. Charles says I'm healthy as a horse. Well, I'm putting words in his mouth because even horses get sick. I do take a couple of pills every day for minor things like cholesterol - who doesn't? But I digress. I was talking about how my doctor treats me, wasn't I?

Just this morning Joseph took me to see Dr. Charles and have some lab work done. Like everybody else, I don't like needles, so maybe I acted out a little bit. Joseph held my hand while the nurse drew two vials of bright red blood from my arm, the same shade of red as Dennis and Joseph's swing. When she was done, she told me to use the cotton ball to keep pressure on the site. I guess I didn't hear her very well, because I tried to get out of the chair. Joseph held the cotton ball in place for a minute. When we left the laboratory, I headed for the yellow exit sign.

"Oh, Mrs. Zifkin, you're going the wrong way. You're in Room Two," the nurse called out as Joseph caught up with me.

"I'm going home," I patiently explained to her. "You got what you needed."

Joseph whispered in my ear, "Mom, the doctor hasn't examined you yet. We need to go to Room Two. Come." He turned me gently around to guide me back down the hall to one of those little rooms with an examination table, two steel frame chairs with dark blue seats, a sink, and a bank of electronic gizmos hanging from the walls.

"Do I need to wear one of those paper dresses?" I asked. I hate those things. They never fit, the ties always rip off, and the room was too cold to disrobe.

"The nurse hasn't laid one out, so I think the doctor just wants to talk about your blood test and some other things," Joseph answered.

"Oh," I said. "What other things?"

"I'm not sure, Mom. It's just a chat to see how you're doing."

I thought about that. As I sat on one of the chairs, I suddenly remembered watching Joseph and his brother playing in the backyard on the shiny new swings my husband had assembled that morning. This morning. It is very colorful. The frame is bright red, the swing seats are dark blue, and there is a bright yellow slide they can ride down. It isn't tall, but then, neither are they.

I was smiling at the memory when a tall man entered the room. "Hello, Mrs. Zifkin, how are you doing?" he asked.

"I'm fine," I answered. "Won't you sit down? Would you like a cup of coffee? And you, young man, would you like some banana bread?" They shook their heads. "No, but thank you for offering," said the tall man very gently.

The room became very quiet. I could hear something humming in the room, one of those gizmos, I suppose. The lights flickered a few times and I fell asleep in the chair. I felt someone catch me before I fell forward. That would have been embarrassing, I thought. I could have hurt myself on this hard floor. Someone picked me up and put me on that hard bed with the ridiculously tiny pillow. There was a lot of hustle and bustle, but I didn't open my eyes so I didn't know who was rushing in and out of the room. The tall man, I believe, was poking and prodding me. The young man whose name is Joseph was holding my hand. "Hold on, Mom, hold on," he kept saying.

You're mistaken, I thought, my boys are four and five years old. Sweet little boys who look like their father, are full of energy, and laugh all the time. They never cry or pout, never have tantrums. They are the best little boys in the world, full of promise. We love them very much and our families do, too. I smiled and wondered what they'll decide to be when they grow up.

A CASTLE IN PARIS

Candice Castle was on the phone with her editor, Denise Kaufman, who had relayed some wonderful news.

"So, Candy," said Denise, "your first book has officially sold fifty-thousand copies in its first run. Congratulations! How does it feel to be a successful travel writer?"

Candy couldn't answer right away. She had known deep inside her books would sell because they weren't run-of-the-mill travel books. Finally, she said, "It feels great, Denise. Now I can pay off my student loans - haha!" At age forty-five, and all but broke in Hoboken, New   Jersey, this was a half-joke.

"Okay," continued Denise. "I'll let you go because I know you're packing to leave for Paris tomorrow. I'm SO jealous! Have a good trip and stay in touch."

As she said goodbye and hung up the phone, Candy sat quietly for a few minutes. Her first book, 'Cookie Callahan and the Mystery of Big Ben' had been set in London, of course. Her second book, already in progress, was titled 'Cookie Callahan and the Mystery at the Louvre'. Although the New York Times had classified her as a travel writer, Candy's books were much more than that. Aimed at the teen market, she planned to write each one in the city where the story took place. Cookie Callahan, the intrepid teenage protagonist who shared Candy's initials, would solve a mystery in each city. Also included in the book was a fold-out map so young readers could follow her as she followed the clues. Years of self-doubt, study, reading, and a burst of determination had resulted in a bestseller. Now she wondered if she could keep the ball rolling around the world.

As she returned to her packing, the phone rang again. "Hello," she answered, while also wondering about where she'd stashed her travel toothbrush.

"Hi, Mom," said the cheery voice on the other end. "Are you done packing?"

Candy laughed. "I'm still in the middle of it. I've never been gone for so long before, so I don't know what to do. I keep putting things in and taking things out of my bags."

"There are shops in Paris, you know," advised her daughter, Kate. "If I were you, I'd just take enough to last a week and if you need more, I'm sure you could find boutiques."

"I'm supposed to write, not shop," Candy laughed again, "even though I'll be in Paris. I have a deadline; have you ever written a book in six weeks?"

"I've never written a book, period," was the answer. "I guess I'm just a little jealous you're going to Paris without me."

"It's just six weeks," assured Candy. "Long enough to get the flavor of the city, spend time at the Louvre and the library, flesh out my outline, and write a first draft for the publisher."

"All work and no play makes Mom the only person who won't take time to sit in a Paris cafe and watch the people go by," warned Kate. "You better get back to packing or you'll be up all night."

"That's okay; I plan to sleep on the plane. It's a long flight."

"Speaking of planes, I'll pick you up at nine so you have plenty of time to get to Newark. See you then. I love you."

"Love you too, honey," Candy said.

Kate was on time the following morning. They loaded her car with a surprisingly small amount of luggage, and hugged before Candy turned her bags over to a porter. "Don't forget to check in with your grandparents," Candy reminded Kate. "Without a computer, they won't get my emails or pictures."

"Will do," Kate assured her. "Have a wonderful time, Mom."

The flight was uneventful and Candy did get some sleep on the plane. When it landed at Charles De Gaulle International Airport, she was happy to see directional signs written in several languages. She headed towards baggage pick-up. Her publisher had arranged transportation to the apartment where she would be staying, and as she saw a man holding a sign reading "Castle", she breathed a sigh of relief. "I'm Candy Castle," she said to him. "I only have this one large bag, plus a carry-on and purse."

The man touched his cap. "Victor Claudel, at your service," he said, lifting her bag. "Please follow me to the limousine."

A limousine, thought Candy. *Ooh-la-la*, she giggled to herself.

Thirty short minutes later, Victor pulled up in front of a lovely building. Her temporary home was a rarity - two bedrooms with a small kitchen, a full bathroom, small living room, and a balcony overlooking several bistros and shops. The apartment belonged to her publishing company and was used for business trips.

Victor got her settled and handed her his business card. "When you need me, Madam, please call."

"Thank you, Victor," she said, taking the card. "I'm going to unpack and acclimate myself today, but tomorrow I plan to visit the Louvre to begin research for my book."

Victor touched his cap. "Your publisher and I have discussed my job as chauffeur, Madam. I will be available essentially any time, as she felt you might get lost in Paris. Au revoir." He smiled, turned and left while Candy watched him go.

Well, how about that? she thought. *I have my own personal chauffeur.*

It was, as far as Candy's stomach clock knew, time for lunch. Looking out the window, she spotted a little bistro across the street. *I'll go down there,* she said to herself, *and see if I can order something.* Grabbing her English to French phrase book, purse and apartment key, she headed to Trois Amis, or Three Friends.

"Bonsoir. Avez-vous de la soupe?" she managed to say in the worst French accent possible to a man she supposed was the manager or owner. He stared at her and said nothing. "Soupe?" she asked again, and mimed eating soup with a spoon. He still said nothing. She looked in her phrase book again.

"Qu'est-ce que vous avez à manger?" she asked, thinking maybe they didn't have soup, but maybe he could recommend something to eat.

The man blinked his eyes, then said, "Madam, I applaud your attempt to speak French, so I will take pity on you." His mustache and goatee fairly quivered with amusement.

Candy gasped and blushed. "I'm sorry," she stammered. "I just arrived from the States, and the only person I know who speaks English is my chauffeur."

He smiled and said, "And now us. My name is Jean, and this is my wife, Marie," he said, indicating a pretty lady sitting at the table. "We don't own this bistro; we are visitors in Paris, also staying in that apartment building. We saw you in the window," he said.

"Oh!" Candy said. "I was airing out the room. I could smell cigarette smoke. I'm not allergic to it, but I don't smoke and it was strong."

"Many people smoke in France. But you need something to eat," Jean said. "Marie, did you enjoy the potato and leek soup?"

"Yes," she answered. "It's very good and hearty. I recommend it. Will you sit with us, Miss...?"

"It's Candace, but Candy is what everyone calls me. Thank you, I would love to join you."

"Our pleasure," Jean said. He turned and caught the waiter's eye. "Garcon, leek soup for the lady," he requested in French. The waiter nodded and returned quickly with a bowl of steamy soup, a sliced loaf of fresh bread, butter, cutlery, and a glass of white wine.

"Oh, I don't drink wine," said Candy. "It makes me sleepy and I have a lot to do today. I prefer water."

Jean shot a quick look at Marie. "The bistro is part of a co-op that produces this wine, Candy. You don't want to offend the owner."

Candy looked at the glass. It was pretty small. "I don't want to hurt anybody's feelings," she said. She took a sip of the wine. It was fruity, not dry, actually refreshing. "I'd better eat the soup while it's still hot," she said, picking up her spoon.

Within ten minutes, the soup, bread and wine were gone and Candy was smiling at her new friends. "That was wonderful. I could eat this every day and be quite happy," she said. Marie beckoned the waiter over to pour them all another glass of wine. At first, Candy put her hand over the glass, but then gave in because, after all, she was in Paris. *One day lost won't hurt*, she told herself. *I'll buckle down tomorrow.*

Many hours later, Candy woke up on her bed. Someone had considerately removed her shoes and thrown the duvet over her. Her eyes felt itchy, her mouth was dry, and she had a headache. It was almost dark outside. *What happened?*, she wondered, startled awake. *I don't remember anything after drinking the second glass of wine. Who tucked me in? I guess it was Jean and Marie. How embarrassing, but I did tell them wine makes me sleepy.*

Candy stood up cautiously and walked slowly to the bathroom to splash her face with water. When she looked for the aspirin in her travel bag, she realized the bag had been moved to the divan, as was her purse. Looking quickly through the items, she realized all of her cash was gone. Thank heaven she'd had the foresight to put her passport and travelers checks in the small wall safe, as she wouldn't be leaving France for weeks and didn't want to risk losing them to pickpockets in the crowds of tourists at the Louvre.

Candy sat down heavily on the divan in disbelief. Jean and Marie must be thieves, she figured. *They said they were staying in this building. I should talk to the concierge to see if it's true. Oh, my aching head! Where's the aspirin?*

Once in the lobby, Candy approached the concierge. He was a middle-aged man, well-dressed, with nice eyes. His name tag read George Breton.

"Excuse me," she said. "I was robbed earlier today and

I need some information about the possible thieves."

The concierge's eyes grew large. "Madam," he said, "are you sure? This is a very safe and respectable establishment."

"Yes, I'm sure," Candy answered. "I know who did it, well, maybe I know, maybe they used fake names. But I could identify them if I saw them."

"We must call the police," Monsieur Breton advised. "They will take a report and perhaps find your thieves."

"Of course, but before we do, do you recall seeing a couple, perhaps in their mid-40s. He is tall, dark, thin, with a mustache and goatee. She is thin, petite with curly, blonde hair. He said their names are Jean and Marie, and they were staying in this building, traveling through Paris."

Monsieur Breton thought. "There is a couple staying here who might fit your description. However, she has long, black hair. She is with her brother who is tall and clean-shaven. They have been here several days, Maria and Juan Artista."

"Artista?" Candy snorted. "That's Spanish for 'artist'. Or maybe 'con artist'."

"I shall call the police to report the incident. Perhaps others have been taken in as well", the concierge said.

Candy blushed with embarrassment. She'd have to tell the police she'd allowed herself to get so sleepy with wine that strangers had taken advantage of her. But at least they hadn't hurt her, and they were nice enough to tuck her into bed. Still, the cash was part of a stipend from the publisher, intended to last six weeks.

Two English-speaking constables came to the apartment to take her statement and description of the suspected thieves. Candy was relieved she hadn't had to go to the police station to do it. After the constables left, she called Victor Claudel to set up her visit to the Louvre the following day.

"Madam Castle, I shall ask my cousin, Maurice, to show you around the Louvre for the day. He is a teacher of English and Art at L'Ecole Sornas, and is very knowledgeable."

"That's kind of you, Victor. My publisher has already scheduled me for a group tour tomorrow at one o'clock, but maybe a personal tour guide would allow me to ask more questions. This is research for a book, after all. Yes, that would be very nice."

"I will call Maurice right away. Don't cancel your group tour until you hear from me, in case he is not available."

Candy agreed and they hung up. Robbery or not, she'd have to get on with the job at hand. This was why she was in Paris. For the rest of the day she worked on her outline, and highlighted phrases she thought would be most useful in her English-to-French book. Then she walked to a bank to cash a traveler's check, and returned to the Three Friends for a light meal of coffee and a small plate of cheese and bread. The book was coming together in her head as she sat in the bistro: Cookie Callahan would overhear someone discussing a plot to steal a valuable piece of art, and that information would help the police uncover a ring of thieves - with Cookie's assistance, of course.

Back in her apartment, Candy wrote furiously for hours, finally receiving a phone call from Victor saying his cousin was indeed free the following afternoon, and would meet them at a certain place in front of the Louvre at one o'clock. Candy asked Victor what Maurice's fee was, he told her, and she thanked him for his kindness. What a lucky break, she thought, then got back to her story.

The following morning, Candy felt better. Her headache was gone, the story was fresh in her mind, and she wasn't experiencing jet lag as much as she thought she would. She was hungry, so she bathed, dressed, left the apartment, and decided to buy some groceries to outfit her kitchen for at least a few days. Charles Breton was at his usual spot in the lobby and directed her down the street to an outdoor market and shops.

"I've brought my phone in case I get lost," she told him.

"If you stay on this street, anyone can direct you back to this building," he said.

Candy walked the few blocks to a charming market where she purchased a pretty bag to carry her groceries, then some fruit, cheese, a box of chocolates, eggs, and a few other things to tide her over. She felt very Parisian when she spotted her reflection in a shop window, the obligatory French baguette sticking out of her bag. *I should take a selfie for the folks back home,* she thought, and did so with the market in the background. Kate would love that, she knew. Then she walked back to her apartment, put her groceries away, and looked at the photo again. But before she forwarded it to Kate, she noticed a few men in the background and one looked familiar.

At twelve-thirty, Victor met her in front of the building and held the car door for her. *I could get used to this,* she thought. *Maybe when I'm a rich and famous author, I'll hire a chauffeur - if there are any in Hoboken.*

They arrived at the appointed spot at one o'clock and Victor spotted his cousin. "Maurice," he said, "this is my employer and friend, Mrs. Candy Castle. Please treat her as you would our grandmother."

Candy looked at him askance.

"I meant, Madam, he should treat you with great kindness and respect, of course," Victor said quickly. "You are not as old as our grandmother, obviously."

Candy laughed. "Stop digging the hole deeper, Victor. I appreciate the intent. Nice to meet you, Maurice," she said. But Maurice did nothing but nod his head and turn his face quickly away to his cousin.

"I will return here at five o'clock," Victor said to them both. "Watch out for pickpockets," he said to Candy, touching his cap as he left..

Candy turned to Maurice. "Where shall we begin?" she asked him, turning around in awe. "This building alone is so enormous."

"What interests you most? Sculptures, paintings, prehistoric art, or masterpieces?" he asked in a whisper. Seeing her questioning face, he added, "I woke up this morning with a bad throat. It pains me when I speak."

"You should have said something to Victor," Candy chided him. "We could have done this tomorrow or I could have taken the group tour."

"Perhaps, Madam," whispered Maurice. "But I have an idea. We will rent electronic tablets and follow the audio guide. I have done so several times and it is quite useful."

"Okay," agreed Candy, "that's fine," but she was thinking she could have done that herself and saved his fee.

They rented two tablets and began the tour. The software allowed them to pause when something caught her fancy, or keep on moving when the items were less interesting to her. But when they got to the exhibit about the art of sketching in Genoa, Italy, which Candy flitted through quickly as the sketches weren't in color, it was difficult to get Maurice to keep up with her. He kept circling around the room. *Oh, well,* she thought, *he's an artist so maybe this is his particular area of interest.*

After an hour or so, she needed to use the ladies room, and told Maurice she was leaving for a few minutes. He nodded and she left, but gasped as she entered the facilities. There, washing her hands, was Marie, or Maria, she was sure of it; petite with curly blonde hair, and wearing the same pretty sandals she had admired the previous day. Candy instinctively turned away when the woman passed her, heading to the exhibit Candy had just left. Ignoring her bladder, Candy followed Marie down the crowded corridor and watched her enter the exhibit. And as Candy expected, Marie walked up to Maurice - or was it Juan or Jean?

Candy watched from behind a pillar and a group of nuns who were admiring some sketches. Marie left in just a few moments, going back out the door, this time turning to the right. After counting to ten, Candy returned to Maurice.

"Thank you for waiting," she said, her voice amazingly calmer than she felt. "But I'm not feeling very well. I think I'm going to call Victor and ask him to pick me up early. I must have eaten something I shouldn't have. Perhaps the wine", she added, looking him in the eye to judge his response.

Maurice spoke with his usual voice now. "Perhaps it was the wine."

"Why did you take my money?" Candy asked quietly. She was feeling brave since they were surrounded by many people, including about a dozen nuns.

"I needed the cash quickly and thought you might have some. Most Americans I have met are wealthy."

"You picked the wrong American. I'm living on a stipend from my publisher, and it's not much."

Maurice shrugged. "I agree we should go, Madam.

Please exit this room and turn to your right."

"I don't think so," Candy said, raising her chin in defiance.

"And why not?" he asked.

"Because I'm standing behind you, cousin."

Maurice stiffened, then turned slowly around. "Victor," he said with a forced laugh. "I should have guessed. Have you followed us all around the museum? Kudos to you. I'm embarrassed for not spotting you."

"Victor, I don't understand what's going on," Candy said.

"This is not the place to discuss the matter. Suffice it to say my cousin and his wife are thieves and are under arrest."

"Marie has left," Maurice stated.

"Indeed. She is on her way to the station accompanied by three undercover police. You'll see her there shortly," answered Victor.

Maurice said nothing, but bowing his head he allowed Victor to lead him without incident into the custody of constables waiting outside the Louvre. Candy followed behind, determined to find out what was going on. There was a great story here and she was going to use it!

After Maurice was in custody, Victor brought Candy back to her apartment. He did not speak in the car, as he was wrapped up in his own thoughts. But once inside, after Candy finally used the bathroom, she made coffee, then offered him some lovely little biscuits she'd bought at the market earlier. Dipping one in his cup of coffee, Victor finally spoke.

"I will explain as much as possible to you, and hope you do not chastise me for using you as, um, bait to catch this fish."

"Bait, really? Okay, I'll save my questions until you're done."

Victor sighed. "Maurice is my cousin; our mothers are sisters. The two of us were close until Maurice decided he did not want to finish school. He dropped out, to his parents' dismay, and went to sea on a merchant vessel. He wanted to see the world. What he experienced was hard work, low wages, and the company of rough, disreputable sailors. He redeemed himself by sketching the crew and places they visited, then later returned to L'Ecole Sornas to get his education in art and eventually taught there. He has made a name for himself."

"I, on the other hand, followed my father's footsteps and became a policeman, then a detective. One of my first assignments in that position was to break up a band of thieves who had stolen some significant art pieces from private homes in Paris. To my horror, I learned Maurice was involved. Fortunately, or perhaps unfortunately, he was not jailed due to a technicality."

"Lately, we began hearing rumors from reliable sources that there was to be a big robbery at the Louvre. Believe me, security there is always high, both electronically and physically. But we had to be sure."

"Where do I come in?" interrupted Candy. "I didn't know anything about this, and I didn't know you were a police detective."

"I have been tailing my cousin for a few weeks," Victor said. "He was meeting with a number of questionable characters, so I knew it would happen soon. With great luck, your publishing house called the police department to see if we could recommend a chauffeur and limousine service to be on call for you, since you knew nothing of Paris. I jumped at the chance because of the connection between you, your desired research at the Louvre, and my cousin's impending plans."

"But Maurice knew you were pretending to be my chauffeur," questioned Candy. "Why did he say he would help you out?"

"I appealed to his ego as an artist and teacher. He didn't think you would identify him if he was clean-shaven. I didn't believe he would harm you, but you were not out of my sight for very long in any case. Until you went to the ladies room," he added with a smile. "I saw you following Marie and you know the rest."

Victor stopped long enough to eat another biscuit and sip his coffee. "You may be asked to testify about the robbery," he added. "Would that bother you?"

Candy thought for a moment. "He and Marie didn't harm me. They put me to bed, even tucked me in, before rifling my bags for cash. They knew the wine would make me sleepy because I told them it would. But before I answer yes or no, let me show you something."

She found the selfie she'd taken in the market with her cell phone, enlarged it, and pointed to three people standing behind her. "You can see the man I thought was Jean talking to two guys, and he's handing one of them a bulky envelope. That could be my money. I realized Jean was Maurice when I saw Marie in the ladies room. I was going to mention it to him today, but you walked up behind him. Does this help you?"

Victor laughed when he saw the photo. "Yes, indeed. Those two are in custody as we speak, claiming they don't know Maurice. Very nice. Perhaps you won't have to testify in person now that we have this photograph."

"It must be awful to have to lock up your own

cousin," Candy said quietly.

"Yes, it is, but he made the choice. His parents will be devastated, and he will lose his position at l'ecole. Perhaps he will serve only a light sentence as nothing was stolen, except for your cash which will be returned to you, and nobody was hurt. My object was to break up the ring, and I think you and my group have done so. The Louvre is safe, at least for the time being."

Candy yawned. "I'm so sorry! I think jet lag has finally caught up with me. I know it's only three o'clock in the afternoon, but I can hardly keep my eyes open."

"Then, Madame Castle, I shall leave. And by the way, although I may not always be available at a moment's notice, you have only to call and one of my men will continue to drive you wherever you wish for the remainder of your stay. We are in your debt." And with that, Victor smiled and left her alone.

I've only been in Paris for two days, thought Candy after Victor left, *and I've already helped stop an art heist. What else could possibly happen to Cookie Callahan in Paris?*

JACK AND THE BEANSTALK

"Jack, it's time for dinner. Jack! Where are you? Are you reading again, you lazy boy? Bring in the mail and come to dinner."

Jack was a dreamer. While his mother called his name multiple times, he leaned on a fence post, leafing through his favorite magazine. He barely registered her voice, his total attention held by a photograph of a handsome, neatly groomed and exquisitely dressed young man wearing snakeskin shoes and carrying a matching briefcase. *Business Style,* his favorite magazine, had just been delivered, and Jack was engrossed in it. Fortunately, a thunderclap brought him out of his daydream and it began to drizzle. "Don't want my magazine to get wet," he yelped, and took off running before the sky opened up.

"It's about time," his mother mumbled as her damp son entered the kitchen. "Go change your overalls and sit down for dinner before it gets cold."

"Yes, ma'am," Jack said as he took a towel from the closet. He dried his hair and changed his clothes. Looking at his reflection in the little mirror, he ran his fingers through his thick, black hair, sighed, and washed his hands before eating.

Mom's soup smelled better than usual. "What's in

this?" he asked, seating himself. "Smells better than usual."

"Maybe it smells better because we've waited so long to eat it," she semi-scolded him. "It's the same soup, but I did find a few mushrooms in the backyard, so I threw those in, too. At least, I think they were mushrooms. Oh, and I traded two eggs for a loaf of crusty bread at the Minute Mart."

Jack ate with reservation (mainly because of the mushrooms) and remained pensive through dinner. Why were they living like paupers when everyone around them could afford the accoutrements of modern living? He knew the lady who ran the Minute Mart paid for the bread out of her own pocket when she swapped it for his mother's eggs. It wasn't really a trade. They weren't living in seventeenth century Europe. His mother lived in a dream world, sure a handsome man would come along and sweep her off her feet. At sixteen, Jack had dropped out of school to help around the farm and prevent her from being committed. His father had left years ago; Jack didn't want to be a homeless orphan so he played along.

But Jack had desires and plans for his future. He wanted to get in on the bottom floor of a start-up IT business, own fifty-one percent of the shares, and live a comfortable life. That's all he wanted. Of course, how he would do that he didn't know, but it seemed like a possibility. So he read magazines about successful young entrepreneurs. He could see himself in those snakeskin shoes, carrying the matching briefcase, wearing Ray-Ban Aviator sunglasses, and stepping onto a private jet to attend a business meeting in Honolulu.

After dinner, his mother cleaned the kitchen and, since it had stopped raining, Jack went out back to see what might be coming up in the garden. Interestingly, nothing would grow back there except pole beans, so they raised several varieties: Lazy Housewife, Scarlet Runner, Romano and Kentucky Wonder. What Jack wouldn't give for potatoes, carrots - even turnips would be a change. Sometimes he wondered if he and his mother would one day succumb to a lack of vitamins.

As he worked his way around the garden, Jack noticed a different vine lying on the ground. He wondered if it was a new strain of pole bean, perhaps crossbred by pollinators. Curious, he left it on the ground and decided to keep an eye on it. He picked some mature bean pods from the Romano, and went inside to get ready for bed.

In the morning the sun shone brightly through his window. Jack was sleepier than usual because he'd stayed up late reading his new magazine. But he woke up instantly the moment he looked out the window and noticed a huge beanstalk reaching to the sky. He couldn't see the top, so he threw on his clothes and ran out the back door, ignoring his mother's greeting.

Where the little unknown vine had lay last night was a hulking, twisted monster of a vine. Jack rubbed his eyes hard, but there it stood, solid as six phone poles tied together. He turned and ran into the house where his mother was flipping beancakes (i.e. ground dried beans fried in a pan like pancakes).

"Mom! Mom! Come outside quick - I have something to show you!" he sputtered.

"Just a moment, Jack," she said. "I have to cook this one just thirty seconds more…"

"Mom, just come!" he cried, grabbing the utensil from her hand, and pulling her towards the door.

"All right, Jack!" she scolded, quickly removing the pan from the stove. "Do you want to start a fire?" But when she saw the fabulous vine reaching skyward from her own garden, she was dumbfounded. "What is it?" she finally breathed.

"I believe it's a hybrid vine," Jack said excitedly. "Cross-pollinated from our four varieties. Isn't it cool?"

"But it wasn't there yesterday," she said. "I couldn't have missed it."

"It was a tiny little thing yesterday," Jack answered with awe. "It grew overnight. Gosh, it's so big and sturdy, I bet you could climb it to the sky."

"Now, Jack, don't get any wild ideas," his mother warned as she shaded her eyes and looked up. "It's awfully high."

Jack said nothing. A giant beanpole, a curious young man, a desire to do something nobody had ever done before - what could go wrong?

"This is very interesting, son, but come eat your beancakes before they get cold," his mother said and walked away.

Jack stood there for another minute, touching the plant, trying to put his arms around it without success. "If it's still here when Mom takes her nap after lunch, I'm going to climb it," he vowed. "Dang, if I had a smartphone, I'd take a picture, send it out on social media, and see if anybody has ever seen anything like this before. But maybe first-hand experience will be better." And with that, he turned towards the house.

An excruciating couple of hours later, after the dishes were washed, dried, and put away, his mother put some beans in a pot to soak before cooking them. Then she yawned, stretched, and said she was going to take a nap. Jack looked up from his book, watched her close her bedroom door, and ran to the garden.

The vine was still there, even stouter than before. Jack went to the giant plant and stepped onto a leaf. He expected it to give way, but it was as sturdy as the rung of a ladder, so he began to climb. It was almost straight up, but he had no fear of falling. He climbed the beanstalk for almost an hour, not looking down.

Just when he was getting very tired and didn't think he could climb anymore, the beanstalk broke through a cloud. Jack gasped when he stepped off the vine onto a huge enclosed metal platform. "Jack," he whispered to himself, "I don't think you're in Kansas anymore."

A noise behind him startled Jack, and he turned to face a large, silvery biped with three very large black eyes. He was even more startled to hear, "Hello, Jack, I've been waiting for you."

"Your, your lips, they didn't move," Jack stuttered.

The creature shook its head and said, "It's called telepathy. Don't you watch cable? It's been discussed on the Travel Channel, Discovery Channel, and A&E. No TV? Whatever - just go with it."

"Where am I?" Jack finally managed.

"You're on my spacecraft hidden by the clouds."

"Whoa! You know me, obviously," Jack said, "but who are you, and what's with this beanstalk?"

"I apologize. My name is Arlo, and this is my latest creation. In two days, you'll be loaded with beans that you can take to the market and sell. Then you and your mother can live a better life. Oh, look, there's a beanpod ready to pop open already."

Jack turned around and looked at the beanstalk. Indeed, a beanpod looked like it was about to open. The problem was, it was the size of a large watermelon.

He looked at the creature with terror in his eyes.

"That beanpod is so heavy, when it falls it will smash into the ground!" mused Arlo. "I didn't think about that. Gravity isn't something we normally worry about. Well, it can't be helped now. You can't stop a force of nature."

"But my mother is asleep down there. She'll be flattened by a rain of giant beans! I've got to go back down there and get her out of the house!"

Arlo stopped him with, "Wait, I'll go with you. I'll cut down the beanstalk once you get your mother far enough away." And with that, they both disappeared from the craft above the clouds, and reappeared in Jack's garden.

Jack didn't have time to ask how that happened. He just rushed into the house and roused his mother from her sleep. After a few frantic moments, she was dressed and they were running towards town.

In the meantime, Arlo materialized a giant axe, and with a few quick chops in the right place, the stalk began to wobble. Beans the size of softballs began raining down on the ground, hundreds and hundreds of them. When the beanstalk itself crashed down, the tremor was felt in town. Many townsfolk thought it was an earthquake and frantically tried to remember whether they were supposed to stop, drop and roll, hold onto their hats, sit in the bathtub, or stand under a doorway.

When the danger was over, Jack and his mother returned to their home. The house hadn't been damaged much as the stalk had fallen in the opposite direction, thanks to Arlo. But there were so many beans and pods, it was difficult to walk.

Jack rubbed his eyes. Was this a dream? That would seem the most likely explanation - until he tripped on a vine. His mother began to cry, but she wasn't sure why.

Perhaps it was the irony of almost dying at the hand (or would that be leaves?) of the very plant that fed them.

"Mom, let's both get some sleep. Don't worry about dinner. If this is a nightmare, it's over now. If it's not, we can deal with it in the morning." He shot Arlo a glance before taking his mother's elbow; Arlo waved and disappeared.

In the morning, the vine was gone but the pods and individual beans were lying all over the place. Jack wondered what to do, but then he remembered his conversation with Arlo in the spaceship. He would sell them! But first he had to get some help moving them.

Jack managed to contact a farm consortium with access to large equipment, which after much negotiation, agreed to sell the beans, giving Jack thirty-five percent of the profits. They also requested an exclusive option to sow the seeds the following year, providing the beans were as profitable as they thought they would be, raising Jack's percentage to forty.

Jack and his mother made enough money to move into town and gradually accumulated all the electronic and other time-saving devices required to live in the twenty-first century. Best of all, when Jack went to work for the consortium, he agreed to wear overalls like everyone else as long as his boots could be snakeskin - and he never ate another bean for the rest of his life.

CHRISTMAS
COOKIES

As she was carefully putting a tray of her famous Christmas cookies in the oven, Birdie Harris's kitchen door flew open. "Don't slam the …!" she managed before the door slammed shut.

Eight-year-old Wylie stopped dead in his tracks. "Oops, Momma Birdie," he said. "I didn't know you was baking."

"Seems all I do this time of year IS bake," his grandmother laughed, turning to scoop the little boy up in her arms. She gave him a big kiss on the forehead. "And how was school today?" she asked, setting him down again.

"Last day of school before Christmas vacation!" he whooped, and hopped around the kitchen with excitement. "Two whole weeks off!"

Birdie smiled at him. "Why don't you go put your school things away, wash your hands, and come back to taste this year's batch of cookies? Then you can tell me if they're better than last year's, okay?"

"Okay!", he agreed, and ran off.

Birdie followed the little boy with her eyes. Wylie still believed in Santa, the elves, flying reindeer and dancing snowmen. But one day he'd learn the truth, and for that she was sorry. Wylie and his thirteen-year-old brother, Tyrell, were her son Marcus's boys. She was raising them while Marcus was in Germany. Their mother, Sheena, was not in the picture, having run off with another man; she didn't like being a service wife and moving all the time. Birdie had wished Sheena good luck. She loved her grandsons and caring for them was no hardship. They kept her busy and were good boys, good company while their daddy was gone.

Wylie shot back into the kitchen. "Okay, I'm ready to taste cookies!"

Birdie laughed and poured him a glass of milk, sat him at the kitchen table, and brought him two different kinds of cookies. "Now you tell me which one you like best," she said.

Wylie smiled and picked up a chocolate chip cookie. It was as big as his hand, nice and soft, and fat with chocolate chips. He took a bite, chewed it slowly, tasting like a fine wine, then proclaimed, "This is the best chocolate chip cookie I ever ate in my life!" He took a sip of milk to cleanse his palate, ready for cookie number two. Birdie chuckled.

The boy picked up the other cookie, a gingerbread man with a smiling face, checkered vest, green pants and red shoes. Wylie's eyes opened wide as he took his first bite; the cookie was slightly crunchy on the bottom but nice and soft on top, exactly perfect. He inhaled deeply to sense the ginger and molasses with his nose. "Momma Birdie, that is SO good! I could eat a lots of these," he finally said. Suddenly serious, he said, "I can't choose which one is better. I love them both."

"It's okay, Wylie," his grandmother said. "It don't matter. I'm just glad you liked both." She looked at the wall clock. "All right, young man," she said. "Please finish your milk and go watch TV for a while. I've got a batch in the oven and one more to go before calling it quits for the day."

Wylie took off for the living room. Birdie smiled after him. The child never walked; he ran everywhere.

She looked at the wall clock again. Tyrell should have been home by now, she thought, and frowned. I hope the bus didn't break down again. But, she reasoned, it was the last day of school before Christmas vacation, so maybe there was a school party that kept the children late. She put the worry out of her mind for now as she removed a batch of peanut butter cookies from the oven, and spooned the last of her batter onto a baking sheet covered with parchment paper. She'd made ten dozen cookies today, most of which were already in Christmas tins.

A half hour went by and Tyrell still hadn't come home; Birdie began to worry. He didn't have a cell phone himself, but when he was with his friends, they'd let him use theirs to call home if he was running late. Wiping her hands on her apron, Birdie walked into the living room and changed the channel on the TV from cartoons to the local news. A lump formed in her throat when she heard the reporter's trained voice catch with emotion.

"Continuing with breaking news, we're here at the scene of an accident where a school bus full of children from Irwin Middle School drove off the road and rolled fifty feet down an embankment. Several emergency vehicles are on the scene to take children to the hospital. Police have advised that the bus driver suffered a non-life-threatening injury and was also taken to the hospital. Stay tuned for more information as we receive it. Now back to the news desk."

Birdie stared at the television set. Her thoughts were running wild. Was Tyrell on that bus? Is he all right or was he taken to the hospital? The smell of something burning jolted her back into reality and she ran to the kitchen to take the cookies out of the oven. They were no good and she'd have to throw them out when they cooled down. She turned off the oven without much thought. Her mind was only on her grandson. She dropped her head and closed her eyes. "Please, Dear Lord," she prayed, "let no child on that bus die. Let them all heal from their injuries." Then she called the police department.

The phone rang several times before someone answered. "Mr. Policeman," she said quietly, "can you tell me if my grandson was on that school bus?"

"What's your grandson's name, ma'am?" asked the dispatcher.

"Tyrell Harris. He's thirteen," she answered. Anxious tears clouded her vision.

"One moment while I check," was the reply. A moment later he said, "Your grandson was taken to the hospital, ma'am. Let me give you the phone number so you can give them a call. Do you have a pen?"

Birdie thanked him, wrote the number on her palm with a pen, then called the hospital, muttering, "Dear Lord, please let my baby be okay."

After a brief phone transfer to the emergency room, a female voice answered the phone. "Triage," she said.

Birdie had no idea what that word was, but she began speaking anyway. "Is my grandson, Tyrell Harris, in your hospital? Is he all right?"

"I'm sorry, ma'am, but we can't divulge that information over the phone due to patient confidentiality."

"But I'm his grandmother!" Birdie wailed. "His daddy's in the army, his mama's run off, and I'm his guardian! I don't have no car and can't call a taxi to this neighborhood after dark, which it is, so you have to tell me or I will go crazy with worry!"

"One moment, please," said the kind voice, and in a minute another voice was on the line. "Mrs. Harris, this is Dr. Tucker. I have information about your grandson, Tyrell."

"Yes, doctor?" sniffed Birdie.

"He has a broken arm and a few bumps and bruises. We're almost finished with the arm cast and gave him a shot for pain. We can send him home with medication tonight if you'd like to pick him up."

Birdie closed her watery eyes, then said, "Doctor, I have no way to pick Tyrell up at the hospital. I don't have no car, and the taxis don't run here after dark. What can I do?"

"Don't worry about that, Mrs. Harris," answered the doctor. "Most of the injured children have been seen, and my shift is over in an hour. I would be happy to bring Tyrell home to you."

"Oh, Doctor, I would be ever so grateful!" cried Birdie.

True to his word, an hour and a half later, Dr. Tucker brought Tyrell home. The boy was drowsy from the medication, and sported a full-length cast on his left arm, a large bandage on his cheek, and one across his nose. "His nose may have bent," the doctor said casually. "It'll look like he went one fast round with Mike Tyson."

Birdie and Wylie wrapped their arms around Tyrell then settled him on the couch. His eyes were drooping, but he said, "That was not a fun way to start Christmas vacation." Everyone laughed with relief; the boy hadn't lost his sense of humor.

Birdie then asked the doctor about the other children on the bus. "Most of them are, or will be, fine like Tyrell," he answered. "There are two children in Critical Care, however."

"I'll pray for them," Birdie said quietly, and the doctor nodded his approval.

Then Birdie's manners kicked in. "Doctor, can I get you anything for your troubles? I'm sure our house is out of the way for you. It's probably not a good idea to leave your car out front too long," she added, glancing at the front door.

The doctor smiled. "I smelled gingerbread when I came in," he said. "My mother used to make gingerbread cookies when I was a little boy and they were my favorite. May I have a cookie?"

Wylie piped up, "They're the best, especially with milk."

Birdie laughed. "I'll get you TWO gingerbread cookies and a glass of milk - or would you prefer coffee?"

"Milk is fine," said Dr. Tucker. "And I would enjoy it more if everyone would join me." He glanced over at Tyrell who had fallen asleep on the couch. "Well, almost everyone," he winked.

As Wylie had proclaimed, the gingerbread men were delicious. The doctor took one of them, wrapped it in a napkin and placed it in his jacket pocket. "For later," he promised. Then he stood up and took Birdie's hand. "It was a pleasure to meet you," he said. "I'm sure Tyrell will feel better tomorrow and his arm will heal in no time at all." He looked at Wylie. "No horseplay with your brother for a month, okay?"

Wylie promised. He even promised to take out the garbage for Tyrell until the cast came off.

Birdie laughed. "That will be a good Christmas present," she said. "Goodbye, Doctor, and thank you from the bottom of my heart."

The doctor smiled. "No, thank you, Mrs. Harris. You reminded me of my mother's Christmas cookies and all she did for us. You see, we lived not too far from here. I went to Irwin Middle School myself and eventually earned a scholarship to medical school. It's been my mission to serve the people I came from. It's a pleasure to end the day with a good memory. Good night." Then he turned and walked out the front door, followed by Wylie.

Birdie clutched the back of her kitchen chair, filled with emotion. She walked over to her sleeping grandson and covered him with a throw blanket, then returned to the kitchen to clean up. Wylie returned, proclaiming, "His car's fine. I think I'm gonna be a doctor, too, and help people."

Birdie opened her arms and they hugged. Then Birdie said, "Time to say goodnight," and walked Wylie down the hallway. A few minutes later, before he climbed into bed, Wylie cocked his head and said, "Momma Birdie, I bet you could heal the whole world with your Christmas cookies."

If only that were true, I would bake twenty-four hours a day, thought Birdie, as she tucked the blankets in around her grandson and turned out the light.

THE AWAKENING

As always, when Lara signed off on the ComBox, she felt a river of emotions flowing through her: sadness, pride, fear, loneliness. The question never left her mind when she spoke to him during their weekly communications: *Are you really my son?*

It was a question for which she probably would never have an answer. Birth records were tightly controlled with only a very few people having access to the data. She was told Yanez was her son on the day she gave birth, and that was that.

After the first twelve hours of his life, Yanez had been removed from her arms. He was raised in typical fashion by bionic pseudo mothers, or SuMoms, tasked with everything from feeding, toilet training, teething, engagement with playthings, and psycho-development. He was then tutored and educated by people whose job was to teach him his designated trade - in his case, bio-engineering - after having been evaluated by placement specialists.

Once a week he and Lara spoke via ComBox and shared ideas regarding magnetism or optics, as well as the music piped in for their entertainment. When they signed off, she would sigh and wonder once again if she was speaking with her actual birth child or a young man to whom she had been assigned.

The ComBox chimed its thrice-daily meal reminder. Lara could have turned it off because she knew the time, but its gentle pinging was melodic. She moved to her eating chamber and pressed the button mounted on the wall. Then she opened the door of the food emulator and removed the tray. She had chosen this meal, as she chose all of them. People were allowed at least this small independence. She had asked for spaghetti bolognese, salad with Italian dressing, a garlic roll, tiramisu for dessert, and hot tea to drink. What the spaghetti, roll, and other items were actually made from was anybody's guess. Everything tasted pretty much the same, but the change in appearance was welcome.

As she ate, she thought about her lesson plans for the following day, as she generally did this time of the evening. She was a teacher of Materials Science and Engineering, specializing in Electronic, Optical, and Magnetic Properties of Materials. Her class consisted of thirty-seven students whom she had never met in person. She was allowed to leave her quarters to utilize the laboratory facilities in one of the teaching rooms in the building. The students would connect via ComBox so they could ask questions in real time. This was how teaching had been done for the past two hundred years. It was convenient, required no traveling, and students could replay the lesson for recall. She had no idea where her students were located.

After eating, she returned everything to the food emulator and pressed the red button which decomposed the contents and returned it to the composter, to be used again and again. As she considered this process and wondered, not for the first time, who had actually come up with the idea to decompose their food, she brushed away the thought that one day her body would probably reach an end like her spaghetti bolognese.

She walked to the study area to arrange her lesson plan and paused to wonder how many of her students were even interested in the information passed on to them. Were they even intrigued by it? Or, she thought with a little shiver of excitement, did they actually enjoy it as she once had? How would they utilize it in their lives? Would they teach or engineer? The answer was unknowable; she could not ask, but only hope, that even one, or maybe a few would follow in her footsteps.

Soon, the ComBox chimed softly, signifying it was time to retire. Lara moved to her sleeping area, changed her clothing, turned out the lights, and fell asleep almost instantly to the sound of sea waves she had never seen but appreciated nonetheless, due to her knowledge of the properties of light and sound.

Yanez aimed a small light down the hallway to locate the sensors. He proceeded slowly and quietly to an area where he had determined the brain case of the building resided. He found no alarms in this housing corridor as few ever considered leaving, having been warned since birth there were dangers to be avoided.

When he had quietly walked several hundred feet, he turned to the right and proceeded down the corridor that led to the teaching rooms. Once again, no alarms sounded. The building was nearly pitch dark to conserve energy. The only lights were his small hand-held device and the blue lights built into the floor every two meters. These lights guided the robots who used the hallways during daylight hours, carrying supplies from one end of the building to the other. At night, the robots were presumably in sleep mode with the other residents of the building.

Yanez stopped in front of the door that opened into the laboratory hallway. According to the plans, this was the hallway he was looking for. He had discovered the plans after one of his educator's classes had superficially discussed this building, designed for its comforts and ease of living. Curious, Yanez dug deeper; one small hint leading to another until he had ultimately been provided with the architectural and engineering layout of the whole building.

Yanez wasn't sure he would find what he was looking for, and it was strictly forbidden to leave the living quarters other than at scheduled times. If you failed to leave or return when expected, one of the little blue-light robots would be sent to look for you.

But so far so good. He touched the laboratory hall door and no alarm sounded. Slowly, he pushed the swinging door open; it wasn't locked. Just inside the door he shone the little beam around, searching for sensors. He walked slowly down the hall, avoiding the blue floor lights in case they did more than guide the robots. His destination was ahead at the end of the hall. His light fell on a rather small box located at knee level. It was transparent so he bent down to look more closely. As he had suspected, the box housed a device that was about the size of his hand. It was black and had small indentations and buttons on its face. Yanez hesitated a moment before opening the transparent box, which was not locked. Was he ethically and morally capable of deciding the future of all the inhabitants of this building?

Yanez's knees shook and his palms were damp. Very slowly he removed the lid from the case and set it on the ground. He knelt down and, with a trembling hand, lifted the item out of its resting place. It weighed very little. Turning it in his hand, he viewed it from all angles. The writing on the item meant nothing to him as far as operation, so he pressed the indent on its face thinking that would activate something.

Indeed, the flat face of the item lit up with ten differently-colored icons, with a large white button on the bottom; obviously, he was meant to choose one. He closed his eyes for a moment, then held the white button down and said the word that would hopefully open this mystery.

"Siri," he said clearly, then held his breath and took his thumb off the white button.

"Hello," a silky woman's voice answered. "How may I help you?"

Yanez's eyes opened in surprise and he almost dropped the device, as he hadn't known what to expect once the button was pushed. He had spent days planning how to get out of his room and to this hallway without detection, but hadn't considered what to ask the brain box. After a moment, he asked, "Where is everybody?" and released the button.

"If you are speaking of humans, all but one are in their designated living quarters at this time," said the voice. "If you are speaking of the Controllers, there are none in this building." Yanez realized he was the human currently not located in his quarters.

"Who are the Controllers?" he asked.

"The Controllers are the sentient mechanisms programmed to protect and maintain humankind after the Great Catastrophe."

Yanez had never heard of the Great Catastrophe; his knowledge of humankind was almost nil. Humans/People were Lara and the eight students to whom he spoke via ComBox. Other than those nine people, only the ubiquitous little blue-light robots seemed to be busy around this building.

Suddenly, not knowing why, Yanez asked, "Is it dangerous for humans to leave this building?"

"No longer. According to the Controllers, the environment outside this building is no longer dangerous for humans," the voice said. "The Great Catastrophe occurred two hundred and eighty-seven years ago. Air, ground, and water contamination were remediated two hundred years ago."

Yanez gasped before continuing. "So the surface of Earth is capable of supporting humans and, I presume, plants. Is that correct?"

"Yes, there are plants, flora to maintain adequate oxygen levels."

"And are there other animals besides humans on the surface of the earth?"

"Yes, there are sentient and non-sentient fauna on the surface of the earth, as well as some just beneath."

Yanez was stunned. He sat on the floor with his back against the wall, eyes filled with tears. What had happened to Earth? Who were the Controllers? Why did he never see another human being although he knew they existed?

"What would happen if I asked you to release all the humans from their living quarters?" he asked.

"As you yourself are now aware, the humans are not locked in. There is nothing to keep them in their rooms other than habit."

Yanez closed his eyes as he asked one last question. "Why haven't the people known all this by now?"

"You are the first to ask."

All these years, generations of people had lived in this very building without meeting each other! After the first eighty-seven years, there were no consequences for leaving their living quarters. They had been cared for by these Controllers, conserved to maintain the species. The people stayed in the building because they were provided with everything, were inspired by nothing, and were curious about nothing.

Yanez stood and replaced the device in the transparent box and closed the lid. Then he walked down the hallway to the end and pushed open the swinging doors. His first inclination was to go back to his own hallway and bang on doors to wake everybody up, to tell them they were free beings, that there was more to their existence than a small, self-contained room which provided everything they needed. However, instead of turning toward his hallway, he followed the blue floor lights to a door marked "Exit". Pushing open the door, he experienced for the very first time in his life, fresh air full of scents and sounds he did not recognize. He gazed with awe at a clear sky full of twinkling lights.

"This is my Earth, too!" he yelled to the sky, the plants, and those animals Siri had mentioned. In his heart, Yanez knew it would take time for his fellow humans to come to grips with this information, learn about their planet, and how to exist on, and with, it. He felt rejuvenated, anxious and eager to become a settler in this new world. There was much to learn, and he was ready! Returning to the building, his body thrummed with excitement. Now it was time to awaken everyone else.

THE BIRTHDAY PARTY

The sound of squealing brakes meant the mailman had come. "There's Mr. Wilson," called out Nora Lee from the bedroom. "Go get the mail, Betty Sue."

It was thirty-six degrees outside, but because her mother needed to keep the house toasty warm, Betty Sue was only wearing shorts, a t-shirt, and flip-flops. She knew she could make the trip from the front door to the street in less than thirty seconds, and decided not to put on her mules and a coat.

But as she began to open the door, Nora Lee's voice rang out, "And while you're outside, bring the dog in from out back. It's the first of the month and you need to give him his flea medicine."

Terrific. Now she had to grab the mail, run around back to get the dog, and bring him inside. Tundra was a big husky who didn't like to go inside, probably because it was so darn hot. He was perfectly content with his insulated dog house and self-filling water bowl.

Okay, thought Betty Sue. *Maybe I'll bring Tundra in first, then go get the mail.* Betty Sue closed the front door and headed toward the back.

As she approached, Nora Lee called out, "Aren't you gone yet, Betty Sue? I want to see if you Uncle Leo sent me a birthday card. Today's my birthday, you know, and Leo always sends a nice card."

"Oh, Momma!" cried out Betty Sue. "For heaven's sake, I can't go in two directions at once. What do you want me to do first?"

There was no reply. Betty Sue was sorry she had expressed her frustration to her mother, especially on her birthday. And Nora Lee was at death's door. Betty Sue took a deep, calming breath and walked into her mother's bedroom. "I'm sorry, Momma. I didn't mean … Momma, where are you going? I'll help you to the bathroom if you need …"

"Now hush," Nora Lee replied calmly. She was sitting on the edge of her bed, smoothing her hair. "I'm going to get dressed, then go out to get the mail. And while I do that, you can bring Tundra in and give him his flea medicine."

Nora Lee went to her closet, brought out a dress she hadn't worn in over a year, shoes, and a heavy sweater. Betty Sue watched and gasped as her mother stepped into the living room and out the front door as though she hadn't been battling pancreatic cancer for many months.

Betty Sue collected herself and watched through the window as her mother walked to the mailbox. She pinched her arm to see if she was dreaming. Although she wanted to keep her mother in her sights until she returned, she had been instructed to give the dog his medicine, so she went to get him. He resisted, of course, but came in reluctantly, lying down on the cool kitchen floor.

"Good boy," said Betty Sue. She didn't know why he didn't like the chewy liver-flavored pills and had to shove them down his throat, then follow up with a spoonful of peanut butter which he did enjoy. Then she let him go back outside where he preferred to be.

Suddenly aware that her mother should have come back with the mail by now, Betty Sue looked out the living room window. There stood her mother at the mailbox, surrounded by several neighbors. All of them were laughing and hugging; it looked like a party without the music and cake. That gave Betty Sue an idea.

Grabbing the red velvet cake she had made as an after-dinner surprise, and a half gallon of Dutch chocolate ice cream, she quickly put the makings of a little party on the kitchen table, threw on her coat, and ran outside before anyone left.

"I'm so glad you're all together. Please come in out of the cold for some birthday cake and ice cream. I'll get some decaf perking."

The neighbors looked at each other. "Whose birthday is it?" asked Mrs. Mendoza, who lived directly across the street.

"It's mine," said Nora Lee. "And I'd be pleased if you would attend," she said with a smile, and nodded to her daughter.

Betty Sue let out a big breath, not realizing she'd been holding it. "Let me help you, Momma," she said, and held out her arm.

"Why, Betty Sue, I'm just fine," said her mother, arching her eyebrows. "I can walk into my own house by myself." And she did just that, surrounded by several old friends she hadn't seen or spoken to in a long time.

Inside the house, everyone headed toward the kitchen. Betty Sue quickly set the table with cups, spoons, forks, cream, sugar - everything necessary for a party. Then she lit the candle on the cake. Nora Lee closed her eyes for ten seconds, then smiled and blew out the candle.

The cake was cut, and coffee and cokes were supplied.

After one woman called her husband, he called a few more neighbors. Before long fifteen people had heard about Nora Lee's birthday party and were standing around in the kitchen, laughing, talking, and hugging. It was wonderful.

An hour later, when the last of the neighbors had drifted home, Nora Lee quietly went to her bedroom, laid the mail on her nightstand, removed her shoes, dress, and sweater, then put on her nightgown and slipped into bed. Meanwhile, Betty Sue had put all the dirty dishes in the dishwasher, threw out the trash, wiped her hands on a dish towel, and walked to her mother's room.

Nora Lee was lying with her eyes closed with a big smile on her face. "Momma," whispered Betty Sue as her heart began pounding with anxiety, "are you okay?" She took her mother's thin hand in her large, warm ones.

"I'm more than okay, daughter, I'm wonderful. I haven't been so happy in a long time. That was my wish you know, to die happy. I'm sorry for any harshness on my part, Betty Sue. That was just the pain talking. Now don't cry, not when I'm happy. I want to see you smile, too."

Betty Sue gulped, then forced a smile. She found it easier when she remembered the crowd of people who had been in this very house not a half hour earlier. "I'm smiling, Momma," she said as she noticed an opened, pink envelope on the nightstand.

"That's good," whispered Nora Lee as she drifted away to her next birthday party.

THE PHOTOGRAPH

It was only noon, but the sky was dark and foreboding. Cowboy-for-hire Jake McCallister had been on his way to Laredo, but it was still twenty-five miles away and he didn't relish the thought of getting himself, or his horse, soaked. A puff of smoke rose up over a hill to his right. "It's either a campfire or a house," he said to Joker, his big Appaloosa. "Let's go check it out." Joker whinnied his appreciation and laid his ears back when they heard a clap of thunder.

It wasn't far to the rise, just a few hundred feet. From the crest Jake saw a few buildings, a saloon, a general store, and a small church. At the end was a blacksmith and livery where he figured he could protect Joker from the oncoming storm. There was no hotel. No matter, he thought, he could sleep in the hay with Joker.

Big drops of rain began to fall and the big horse tossed his head. "Okay, let's get to the livery stable first and dry you off, you big marshmallow. Don't want you to melt in the rain." Joker picked up his pace and in a moment they were outside the livery. Jake led the horse in but didn't see anyone.

"Anybody here?" he called out, but there was no reply. Ting, ting, ting he heard. "Sounds like a blacksmith to me. Probably on the other side of the wall." He walked around to the other half of the building but there was nobody there. The forge was out; it wasn't even warm.

A chill ran down Jake's spine but he brushed it off as being cold from the weather. He could hear the wind picking up, as a fierce storm began to rage outside. "Made it just in time," he thought. "Well, let me see if there's anything for Joker to eat and I'll pay the blacksmith later."

But Joker had already found a full bucket of oats, and a manger held a good amount of dry hay. He was content. Jake removed the saddle and wiped his horse down, then threw a blanket over him. While he pumped some water into the dry trough, he thought back to his first impressions of the little town - if you could call it that. He hadn't seen or heard anything or anybody, not even a bird. So, after putting Joker in a nice, warm stall, he put on his poncho, pulled his hat down low, and went out to check the other buildings.

The wind almost knocked him into the side of the building and his boots sank up to his ankles in sticky mud already forming on the dirt street. Cursing, he continued on his way, boots squelching, until he reached the covered area outside the general store. Grateful for cover, he stamped his muddy feet on the boards, then tried the door. It wasn't locked and the doorbell jingled merrily when he entered.

"Hello!" he hollered out. The store was well-stocked with provisions, the floor was swept, windows clean. A bell on the sales counter caught his eye, so he tapped it several times. No response. Taking a deep breath, Jake removed his dripping poncho and hung it on a nail. Then with some trepidation, he walked to the back of the store, his jingling spurs being the only sound in the place besides the pounding of his heart.

As with the stable, there was nobody in the back. The little kitchen was clean but the wood stove was cold, although a pile of wood chips and logs were cradled nearby. He walked behind a screen and saw two cots, made up neatly; nobody was sleeping in them.

Jake backed up into the kitchen. "Where in tarnation is everybody? If it wasn't raining cats and dogs, I'd get back on Joker and leave pronto," he whispered to himself.

And then he heard it - the sound of an old ragtime piano and voices laughing, glasses clinking. Jake breathed a sigh of relief. There were people in the saloon. Everybody must be there, he decided. His heart rate subsided. "Sounds like the storm's letting up a little. I'll go walk to the end and pay for Joker's feed, maybe get myself something to eat and drink."

Putting his clammy poncho back on, Jake headed to the saloon, staying close to the buildings in order to walk on the boards. Music and laughter were getting louder and his fears abated. *The Raven Saloon* was painted on the window over a silhouette of a large black bird.

He opened the door and immediately the sounds vanished as Jake entered a room empty of people. Walking slowly around the room, he looked into every corner and behind the bar. The bar was stocked with alcohol and beer. He considered having a shot to calm his nerves.

He walked to the rear of the saloon - nobody was there. "I must be going crazy," he decided. "I know I heard voices and noises. Maybe this is all a nightmare." He smacked his hand on the bar hard, bringing tears to his eyes. He saw a photograph on the wall behind the bar and examined it carefully. It was large, about three by five feet, and depicted this little town in sepia tones. Everything was the same except there were people - dozens of people - standing on the street facing the camera. Children, shopkeepers, farmers, and a blacksmith. There were horses, carts and wagons, even a dog here and there. Under the photograph were the words "Wheatfield, Texas, 1871". It had been taken by a photographer named Max Underland.

Suddenly, Jake began to breathe in spasms. He clutched his chest and cried out to an unseen party, "No! I don't want to go!" before falling to the floor dead.

If you are unfortunate enough to come across Wheatfield, Texas while riding your horse, you will see a building next to the saloon. It is not in the photograph. The sign on the window reads "Undertaker - Maxwell Underland, Proprietor". And if you are brave - or foolish - enough to enter The Raven Saloon, take a look at the large sepia photograph behind the bar. In the lower right-hand corner of the picture is a cowboy on an Appaloosa horse. I suggest you leave immediately.

MAMMOTH'S GREAT LIFE

by Logan Davies

I am an old man now, but my brother and I were very young men, boys really, when we started running the family plantation. Pop and Momma stayed in Fayette County for a while until they could wrap things up and move to the farm, so brother James and I had our ears to the ground, regularly talking to farmers, seeking advice about how to work the place for a profit.

Pop's daddy, Zachariah, had left us boys some money with which we purchased a jack donkey for a good price in Kentucky. He was a big boy. His daddy, also named Mammoth, was a stud, siring dozens of mules over his long life. Our Mammoth was young, just five, and we hoped he'd do the same, make us rich.

We wrote up a legal flier, had a hundred printed off in Memphis, and hung them everywhere we could.

The Renowned Jack - MAMMOTH - will stand the remaining part of the season commencing April 16th and ending June 10th, 1840, at our stable, 7 miles east of Bartlett, 3-½ miles south of Brunswick, 1-½

*miles west of Morning Sun, and will serve mares at
$10 by the insurance, $8 for the season, and $6 for
the leap. Money is due when the fact is ascertained
or property transferred, with a lien on the foal for
service. All care will be taken to prevent accidents,
but will not be responsible for any that may occur.
DESCRIPTION AND PEDIGREE: Mammoth is a dark,
iron gray, nearly black, 15 hands high, Jack measure,
well-formed and very heavy. He was sired by Old
Mammoth of Kentucky, his dam was a Jennet of the
celebrated General Wool stock. L.E. & J.B. Davies.*

We didn't sit back on our heels though, waiting for
everyone to bring their mares and jennies - oh, no. We
worked the farm alongside the help doing everything. The
only exception was cooking because we were fortunate
to have two women who did the cooking and baking for
everybody. They were Trilly and Mercy, sisters who had
managed to stay together by the grace of God and two good
masters. Their husbands worked the fields and were also
handymen who showed us the ropes, too. We worked hard
to stay afloat and make our parents proud.

I recall one evening after dinner was done, Mercy
went to the kitchen to bring in a dessert. We didn't always
have dessert, but this was a special occasion - James' 13th
birthday - and Mercy had made his favorite pecan pie. In
fact, she had made two of them because, well, because
he was her favorite. I'm not jealous about that, as Trilly
favored me. But I digress.

Within seconds of the dishes being taken away by
the sisters, we heard an awful shrieking from the kitchen.
All of us jumped up and ran into the next room to see what

was going on. Mercy and Trilly were hollering and flapping their aprons at the mostly empty pie safe. When all was said and done, it appeared that Mammoth had smelled the pies as they were cooling, was sorely tempted, and managed to get out of the barn. As his luck would have it, Trilly and Mercy had gone out to the well and everyone else was hard at work when he kicked the door open and got at the pies. This was our first evidence of his being a strong and resourceful jackass. To wrap up this story, we stuck a candle in an apple and let James blow it out while we all sang the birthday song. Mercy said he'd have to wait a while before he got another pecan pie.

We never figured out how Mammoth got out of the barn. I had closed it myself, threw the latch, and checked it as usual. We guessed he just watched and figured it out for himself, because no matter how many times he got out, there was never any damage to the door. Most evenings, though, after a day's work - either plowing, hauling, or siring - he was content to stay in his stall munching hay. I say most evenings because he did occasionally tire of eating and sleeping, desiring a little more mental stimulation. It must have been a game for him. He didn't escape often enough for us to make major changes to barn security, though, as we needed quick access in case of an emergency.

One day, while we were holding a beautiful chestnut mare for the season, Mammoth figured out how he could double his pleasure. He scuffed a rock close enough to her stall door and pawed a dab of manure on it so we didn't see it when we latched the door at the top with a strap. That night, he let himself out of his own stall, stepped up on the rock to give himself more leverage, and worked the strap off her door. He had a grand time that night. In fact, the poor boy was so tired the following day, it was all we could do to get him out of the stable. It only took a quick look around to figure out why.

Jackasses can be stubborn, and when they make a decision not to do something, there's not much you can do to change their mind. It's a matter of psychology; you have to make them think that your request is their idea. One day, towards the end of the season, Mammoth decided not to participate in the day's activities. Nobody knew why; he hadn't even left his stall that night, and had gotten a good night's rest. But as I said, jackasses are stubborn. Suddenly, I remembered his fondness for pecan pies. Mercy hadn't made one since, even though we'd asked several times. It's not like we didn't have pecans - there were bags of them stored away from squirrels - but she had been very upset by the incident, I supposed.

I went to the cellar and found a ten-pound bag of pecans. James and I attached it to the plow, then we had a few hands get it over to the stable. Mammoth's head shot up and his ears stood on end - he could smell those pecans coming closer and closer. The barn door was already open, and when James opened the stall door, don't you know that jackass took off running towards the plow! I never saw him move so quickly. We had found his weakness. Long story short, after he finished off the pecans, Mammoth decided since he was already standing there, he may as well help us plow another patch for the vegetable garden. As long as we had pecans, we could get some work done. I was real proud of myself for thinking up that solution.

Just before the cold weather set in, Pop and Momma moved to the plantation, their business done in Fayette County. They were very proud of the work and improvements we had made to the place, not to mention the money made from Mammoth's stud fees. He had managed to cover thirty mares and jennies - an impressive number - and most of them had carried full term. Our parents couldn't believe some of the stories we told them about Mammoth; they thought we were making up tales. But it was all true. We had an easier winter 1840-1841 because of that jackass, that's for sure.

When the spring of 1841 rolled around, and James and I were in Bartlett Station one day picking up supplies, we ran into the farmer from Kentucky from whom we had purchased Mammoth. We shook hands and he asked us how things were going. We told him a story or two, and said we felt really blessed to have such an interesting helper around as was Mammoth. The farmer - Mr. Lawson, was his name - sucked on his cigar and blew out a cloud of smoke, saying nothing for a minute. Then he tucked his thumbs under his braces and swayed back and forth, smiling, then laughing out loud. As we stood there gawking at him, he said, "Boys, I'm sure glad you figgered that jack out, and what makes him tick. I don't doubt your tales one little bit. He's smarter than a lot of folks I know. In fact, that's why I sold him to you at a loss. He'd gotten the best of me a few times and I just couldn't live with an animal that's smarter than me, and that's the truth. His daddy is a big bag of muscle and drive, but young Mammoth, I think he got his smarts from his mama and her association to the celebrated General John E. Wool, who fought in every war since the War of 1812. It was said that when the general was home on his New York farm, he would go to the barn for peace and quiet and talk out his plans to the livestock. Who knows what animals were educated and inspired by his commanding presence?"

"Haha!," my brother laughed. "Tell me another!"

But you know what? I believed Mr. Lawson. He told

a realsome story and didn't gain anything from it. All I know is what I observed these past few months, and what I learned was when somebody sets their mind to do something, stand back, whether they're a person or a stubborn jackass.

THE ACTRESS

(Inspired by "Charwomen", Saturday Evening Post cover (April 6, 1946) by Norman Rockwell)

The first time I stepped onto the stage as a non-speaking maid in a successful Broadway play, I felt I'd made the big time. I was seventeen years old. During that run, I must have curtsied about a thousand times. Oh, how I wished I could have at least said, "Yes, madam," but the director frowned on it. He'd have to pay me extra for a speaking part, you see.

My aunts, Gertrude and Hilda Nussbaum, were my biggest fans. They had followed my career as an actress, giving me pointers along the way.

"Don't let the others upstage you," reminded Gertrude. Being upstaged was a trick actors played on those less experienced. When an actor moved farther to the rear of the stage than you (i.e. upstage), you had to almost turn your back on the audience which made it hard for them to register your expression or hear you.

"Don't look right into the spotlight," warned Hilda. "It'll blind you, then you'll walk into something, or off the stage."

Obvious observations, but well-intended, and accumulated over many years of cleaning the Empress

Theater. They had met numerous stage actors and performers, knew the stage, lighting, construction, and wardrobe crews, and listened in on all the gossip. Gossip was an art form at their apartment building. Most folks had a radio in 1930, but there was no television, so chatting and visiting was their usual form of entertainment.

In this apartment, the spinster sisters could always come up with an anecdote or bit of gossip to share. The other tenants would hear their stories and exclaim how fortunate they were to work in such a colorful environment.

As I said before, I considered myself a professional actress at seventeen, but I'd done a considerable amount of singing and dancing since the age of six. While my parents struggled to keep their large family afloat on a single salary, my aunts, who had no dependents, decided to pay for my acting, dancing, and singing lessons. I didn't realize what that had cost them in time, money, or self-sacrifice until I was much older.

My big break came when, at the age of twenty-one, I was chosen to sing and dance in a revue show called Garrick Gaieties. I sang, tap-danced, and had one comedy skit with Harvey Whitman, considered at the time to be the funniest man on Broadway. Happily, for my aunts, the show ran for six months at the Empress Theater, although Aunt Gertrude warned me about Harvey. "He's a two-timer," she told me. "Keep it professional." I took her advice, and Harvey eventually ran off with another actress, leaving his wife and children behind. As I said before, my aunts knew everybody and heard everything. I didn't question them.

The years went by and Broadway was kind to me. I worked hard and enjoyed the money, celebrity, and being recognized in the street and in good restaurants. I even won a couple of Toni awards. Through the years my aunts continued to praise me, knowing they'd had a part in my success.

Twenty years went by very quickly. I was still in my prime as an actress and had moved from New York to Los Angeles where my movie career took off. It was during this hectic time that I somehow forgot my beloved aunts. Oh, I always called them on their birthdays and holidays, and if I was in New York, I tried to set aside time to see them, although I couldn't always make that happen because of my tight schedule.

The years rolled along. One night I received a phone call at two-thirty in the morning. I fumbled for the phone and answered the insistent ringing with a very loud "Hello". After a few seconds, I heard someone sniffling on the other end of the line and instinctively knew who it was. "Hello," I said more gently.

"Jenny," the old voice whispered hoarsely, "this is Aunt Gert. I'm sorry to call so late; I forgot you're three hours behind us and would probably still be asleep. But," she paused, "I wanted you to know that Aunt Hilda passed away yesterday, that's all."

That's all? I was horror-struck and embarrassed. I tried to recall the last time I had phoned - maybe a month or six weeks ago around Easter. And it had been a quick call because I had to get on a plane and hadn't packed yet. Tears welled up in my eyes.

"Oh, Aunt Gert," I cried. "What happened?"

"Well, she's had a few minor ailments like heartburn, muscle strains, and so forth for quite a while. At least we thought they were minor. Turns out she had a bad heart and we had ignored the symptoms."

I couldn't speak, my heart was in my mouth.

"At least she died in the theater," said my aunt, "just where she would have chosen. She was picking up Playbills, then sat down and just passed away in C-7. Best seat in the house."

And then Aunt Gertrude began to laugh and I had to laugh with her. We continued for a few minutes, fueling each other, laughing at the irony. And I now knew what to say.

"Aunt Gert, I want you to come to California to live with me. The weather is mild, you won't have to fight with the snow in winter, and I can introduce you to some movie stars - Judy Garland, Bing Crosby and Bob Hope, Maureen O'Sullivan, Cesar Romero, Rita Hayworth, Doris Day, and Rock Hudson. Maurice Chevalier is my next-door neighbor. I'll cancel some television appearances, come to New York for the funeral, and help you pack. What do you say?"

I didn't hear anything but breathing from the other end for a few seconds while she considered my proposal. Finally, she said, "I've lived my whole life in New York City and only had one job the whole time because Hilda and I wanted to stay together. But now she's gone and doesn't need me anymore. Yes, Jennie, please come and help me send her off with a big party. And then I'll go to California with you. I will desperately miss my sister, but I think she'd tell me to go. After all, how often does Maurice Chevalier get to New York? I'll never meet him unless I go to California."

Within a few weeks, the circle was complete. I was now caring for my aunt who had sacrificed so much to support me. In time I introduced her to every star and celebrity I could. And my handsome and charming next-door neighbor came over often for lunch or drinks - just to

IRENE BECKER

gossip.

OLLA MAE

It was a miserable, misty night and the wind had picked up now that the sun was setting. Olla Mae Bouche pulled her old coat tighter around her as she waited for the bus. When it slowly rolled to a stop, she stepped up wearily, deposited her fare, and sat down heavily behind the bus driver. She put her large handbag on the seat next to her and removed her plastic rain bonnet. The bus was half-empty this evening; maybe the rain had kept people from going downtown today.

With a sigh, she slipped her tired feet out of the white work shoes she'd been wearing since five a.m. and wiggled her toes. The shoes were old and the arch supports had worn out long ago, but she couldn't afford to spend fifty dollars on a new pair of shoes right now. Or ever, it seemed. There were always other, more important things to spend her money on.

Olla Mae closed her eyes and tried to relax for the remainder of the trip home. She had ridden this bus route for decades and all the drivers knew where she got off, even if she fell asleep. She willed her scalp to relax, her eyes to relax, her mouth, jaw, neck, shoulders, and arms. By the time she got to her lower back, the driver turned to her and said, "Miz Bouche, you're home. Don't rush, I'm ahead of schedule," he smiled at her.

Olla Mae opened her eyes and slipped her shoes back

on, donned the rain bonnet, then gathered her handbag. She stopped at the front of the bus, turned to the driver and said quietly, "Thank you, Mr. Douglas. It was a very gentle ride and I appreciate it."

"Good night, Miz Bouche," he answered. "I hope you don't get too wet walking home."

Olla Mae just smiled at him. Her apartment was four blocks off the main road and she would no doubt be soaked to the skin by the time she got there.

As she began walking home, Olla Mae removed her false teeth and put them in the pocket of her coat. They had been slipping for half the day and were uncomfortable. She didn't need them anymore tonight. She'd made a big pot of fresh vegetable soup on Sunday which would last her through the week, and it didn't require much chewing.

She finally arrived at her building and entered the small, dimly-lit lobby. After checking her mailbox and finding nothing but advertisements, Olla Mae pushed the elevator button. Twenty-five years ago, she'd had to walk up the four stories to her apartment but, thankfully, the elevator had been installed about ten years ago.

Her apartment was chilly; the heat hadn't been on all day. She turned the thermostat up a little. It would take a few minutes to warm up the apartment. In the meantime, she knew heating her soup would take the chill out of the small kitchen. She took the soup pot out of the refrigerator and put it on the burner, setting it to medium. Then she used the bathroom, washed her hands, changed from her damp uniform into a bathrobe too big for her, and set the table for two. For her and Ike, just like always.

While she waited for the soup to heat, she began talking to the empty chair across from her. "I'm sorry I had to use your bathrobe, Ike, but my clothes were pretty wet. Shoes, too. Hope they all dry out overnight. But pretty soon it will be spring and the flowers and trees will start to bloom. I'm fixing to plant more herbs this year out on the balcony - basil, mint, parsley, rosemary for sure. I might even try a cherry tomato again, although last year's didn't do too well, did it? Oh, hold on, I think the soup's ready."

Olla Mae stood up and looked into the pot which rolled with little waves of spinach crested with sliced okra and lentils. She turned to the table. "It's ready," she said, picking up his soup bowl. She dipped a ladle into the pot and brought up a nice helping, then placed it on the table by the empty chair. Then she ladled out a serving for herself.

Sitting down, she tucked the cloth napkin into the top of the bathrobe, then bowed her head. "Thank you, Lord, for what we are about to eat, Amen." She took a sip to make sure it wasn't too hot, then said, "It's just right, Ike, you can go ahead."

As she ate, Olla Mae continued her previous conversation. "What was I saying? I think it was about vegetables. Oh, yes, tomatoes," she smiled toothlessly. "I'll have to read up on them before planting another one. Maybe they need different soil than what I used last year."

Olla Mae paused as if she was listening. "Well, that's a topic for another day. Are you done? She picked up Ike's bowl and dumped it back into the pot. "Waste not, want not," she admonished the chair. "I need to clean my dentures now before I forget. Gotta clean them or I can't talk to people. I can only talk to you without my teeth, Ike", she laughed. "Wish I was an alligator sometimes so I'd have lots of teeth to chew my food up good and not spit when I talk."

She retrieved her teeth from the pocket of her coat and took them into the bathroom. After a light brushing, she put them in the container with a denture tablet. "I'm running out of Polident," she said. "Better put that on the shopping list."

After cleaning up the kitchen, Olla Mae put her nightgown on as well as her warmest, fluffiest socks, a Christmas present from her friend and neighbor, Wanda Jackson. "Wanda is a very nice person," she said as if her husband was standing in the bedroom with her. "I wish she could find herself a good man like you, Ike. It's a real shame she lives all alone." She sighed deeply. "I was gonna watch a little TV, but you know, I'm pretty weary tonight. Hope you don't mind if I go to bed early. No pillow fighting tonight, Ike," she winked. "Maybe tomorrow."

Moments later, Olla Mae was asleep. The apartment became very quiet, and the only sounds were those an apartment makes at night - the bubbling and clicking of a radiator, the refrigerator humming, the creaking noise that floors make when someone in an apartment above walks across their room. Then a feather floated through the air, bobbing up and down on an invisible current. It circled the bed twice before finally coming to rest on the floor. And if you were listening very hard, you could hear light-hearted laughter as if a young couple had just had a pillow fight and fallen onto the bed and into each other's arms. Good night, Olla Mae, sleep well.

SPECIAL DELIVERY

Willis and I were sitting at the console of our little pod, not speaking. I had just set the coordinates for Coros 5 where we were to pick up a package for delivery to Coros 12. I wondered why they couldn't find a local carrier to hop just half a parsec - why hire a Federation Express pod? I had felt uncomfortable about taking the little job because in our experience, it was the little ones that were the most trouble. But a job's a job, credits are credits, and that was that.

I'd brought Willis with me again because I dislike traveling alone. Sometimes, as quiet as space travel is, you need someone to talk to, some kind of noise to stimulate your ears so you don't start thinking you're going deaf. Most of us space jockeys talk and sing to ourselves. Unlike other people, we like to recreate where there are lots of folks around, needing a break from solitude.

I'd read up on the Coros System, a nice yellow sun named Coros Prime surrounded by an unimaginatively-named group of planets numbered Corus 1 through Coros 13. I wondered if these people didn't have deities to name their planets after. I'll have to look it up one day. But it works for them. Some of the planets are not habitable by our standards, but there are a few blessed with oxygen, hydrogen, and the essential minerals needed for humanoid life forms.

Upon landing at Coros 5 Station 6, I powered down and checked in with Station Control.

"Federation Express pod Alpha six-two-three, provide your credentials," someone said, and I beamed them over. Normally, credentials check only took about ten seconds, but we waited a few minutes. That made me curious.

"Federation Express pod Alpha six-two-three, you may leave your craft."

"Thanks," I said, wondering what the hold-up was about. The place wasn't bustling or crowded; in fact, we were the only craft on the ground. Interesting.

Willis and I walked to the terminal. It felt good to stretch my legs; I almost wished it was a little farther away. When I was hired on to Federation Express, I was almost too tall to fit into the craft because of my long legs and arms. But they were in dire need of express jocks, so my chair was refashioned, and soon I was flying. That was twenty years ago; somebody at Federation Express owes me a gold star for my commitment to the company. Better yet, a raise.

Inside the station, it was cool and humid. On some planets, you'd say it felt like rain was on the way. A little strange for me, but not for the Station Master who met us as we entered the door. He was scaly and smelled a little fishy, which explained the atmosphere in the building. I probably didn't smell too good, either, come to think of it. We'd been delivering for five days straight and the pod offered no personal hygiene setup except for the basic essentials.

Although I was hoping we would spend at least a few hours on Coros 5 to give us time to freshen up, sleep lying down, and clean out the pod, the Station Master seemed intent on speeding us on our way. He was holding a locked box, oblong in shape, made of a lightweight metal drilled through with tiny holes, and which glinted under the artificial lights as he nervously shifted it around. With a slightly nervous, high voice, he said, "This is the package you must deliver to Coros 12. Coordinates have already been uploaded to your pod. Please sign here and here on this form ... right, thank you." He thrust the box at me. "I wish you a safe journey."

Again, I was struck with the oddness of events. I felt an involuntary shiver as if a ball of frozen H20 had run down the back of my uniform and was melting into my undergarments. Something was off. I looked at Willis who returned my look with his beady eyes.

"Sir, before we leave, may we have a few minutes to, er, attend to personal hygiene?" I asked as politely as I could.

The Station Master swayed a little before he agreed. "I'm very sorry for my rudeness," he said. "The hygiene area is over there." He pointed to his left. "But please hurry. The need is urgent."

"So is mine," I answered, walking briskly in the direction he had pointed. Willis came with me.

Once we were behind closed doors, I set the box on a table to examine it. The box was ordinary, pretty typical for deliveries, but it had an odd smell. Rather, it had a nice floral smell. I picked it up and shook it a little. Nothing exploded, thankfully. Then I put it to my ear and heard "zzz". Startled, I set the box back on the table. Willis and I took a moment to attend to business, then we left the hygiene area with the box under my arm, bade goodbye to the Station Manager and two guards at the door, and returned to our pod. After checking the coordinates, we powered up and set off for Coros 12.

In Earth time, it took twelve minutes to travel the short distance. After landing, we went through the same security measures as before, then walked into the station, the box cradled in the crook of my arm. We entered as instructed and stopped in the lobby, whereupon a second Station Master of the same species, and a female with large eyes, approached us.

"Welcome, welcome," the Station Master declared, a bit too cheerily, apparently trying to impress the woman. "Thank you for bringing the package so quickly. Once you hand it to me, you may leave. See the secretary at the door to receive your credits."

"Just a moment, please," interjected the woman as I stepped forward. "I have a question or two. Did you open the box?"

Her question almost offended me. "No, ma'am, that is against our rules. I confess I smelled it and jiggled the box a bit, then heard a buzz which concerned me a little, but I did not open the box."

She stared into my eyes, tilted her head, then smiled. "I believe you," she said. "You and your, er, friend may leave now."

As she turned away, I cleared my throat unnecessarily, then said, "Ma'am, I just have to ask what is in the box. I've never asked anyone before, but I feel very deeply that I must this time. Of course, if it's a secret, I understand."

She stopped and turned, then said, "Very well. You have delivered into my hands the savior of Coros 12. She is, in fact, a queen bee, attended by several drones. You see, a disease eviscerated the bee population here a few years ago and, as a result, our crops began to die. We eat no meat, therefore this was a tremendous blow for us. Even in this wonderful climate, without cross- pollinators, we are a doomed society. Does that satisfy your curiosity?"

"Yes, ma'am, it does. Thank you for the explanation, and I am truly sorry I shook the box a little. I hope it didn't upset or harm Her Majesty, and I wish her a long and fruitful life."

The woman was silent for a moment, then said, "She understands your curiosity. Now I must take her and her attendants to their new hive. It has been a pleasure." She turned and walked away with the Station Master hurrying beside her.

I sighed and walked to the secretary who took my credit card and loaded an enormous number of credits onto it. I was surprised but said nothing, just smiled at the lady, and we walked out the door to our pod.

"Willis, that was the most interesting delivery we have made in twenty years," I said. "I think we deserve a day off. Let's go back to Coros 5 and check into a spa. I've got to send you through the washer-dryer. You're pretty filthy, and I need some different sort of company, no offense."

It's a good thing sock puppets don't talk back. I'm sure I would have gotten an earful.

LUCINDA

The river near ran dry that year. We all knew why. It was all because of Lucinda and her witchy ways, that's what we know for sure. I stood on the bank, lookin' at the mud sloshin' in the riverbed, a few brave ripples reachin' up for the sky, beggin' for more water, more strength. The river didn't want to die. It had a job to do, to push on south and provide water for crops, folks, and animals.

I had no reason to wade in, but I did. I took off my boots and sat down on the bank, danglin' my feet over the edge. The year before, this alone would have cooled my legs all the way to the knee. This year, I'd need to jump out a ways to keep from slidin' down the embankment, so that's what I did. I slipped in the mud but didn't fall. The water only touched my shin bones.

Daddy had said that very morning he would try to dig another well as he had nothin' else to do with his day, seein' as our crops was dryin' up. Momma cried when he said that. First Lucinda'd stopped the rain, then she killed the crops, and then she disappeared.

I sloshed and skid down the middle of the river, thinkin' about Lucinda. She was a strange one. Momma said she was like that all her life. She was older than me by eight years, and I recall her talkin' to the plants and trees, plantin' goldenrod around for the bees to make honey, drawin' pictures in the sand or on the walls of our room with charcoal. Momma said they didn't know where she learned that; we had no neighbors or kin for miles around.

The river came to a right-hand bend and I continued on, feelin' the mud, stones and grit ooze between my toes. The water, what there was of it, was warm and the sun was hot. I was lost in my thoughts when I saw a big jumble of branches, twigs and other stuff the river had carried down as far as it could before it stopped flowin'. But as I neared the jam, I spied a bright yellow color in between some of the tree limbs. Curious, I went over to see what it was. It was the bottom of a yellow dress, torn off. And then I seen an arm and stopped walkin' suddenly, almost fallin'. My hands begun shakin' and I screamed loud. I couldn't help it. I knew it was Lucinda from the bright yellow dress and her lanky arm.

Not wantin' to see any more, I scrambled out of the river and ran towards the cabin, leavin' my boots up river where I'd left 'em. I needed my parents more than my boots. Out of breath, I found Momma hangin' laundry on the porch rail. I ran to her and buried my face in her apron, cryin' hard.

Momma held me tight. "What's the matter, child? Tell me what happened." And I told her what I seen.

Only a minute later, after she called to Daddy, we all three went as quick as possible to the jumble of branches and twigs on the far side of the river where I seen Lucinda's arm and her yellow dress. Daddy jumped in, boots and all. We watched in horror as he heaved branches like a giant man to uncover the remains of his daughter. I saw him kneel in the mud, cryin' like a little child, heard him sayin', "I'm sorry, I'm so sorry," over and over.

I hadn't noticed Momma, who had set down on the ground a few feet away from me. Her eyes were bugged out, her face white as a ghost, but she made no noise. As Daddy rose from his knees after pickin' Lucinda up, a few tears trickled down her face.

"I knew," she whispered. "I knew she was dead, not run off. For all our fallin's out, we still loved her and she knew it. She woulda come home one day."

They took her home slow, after sending me to get my boots first. When I got back to the cabin, they had laid her out on the table. Momma was cleanin' her up, and Daddy had the spade in his hand as he walked out back to dig another grave. There were already two smaller ones for the babies that hadn't lived long, the ones who died between Lucinda and me. My heart felt like it was bein' squeezed by a rock. I suspect Momma and Daddy's hearts felt purty much the same.

After Daddy had dug the grave and they wrapped Lucinda in a sheet, she was laid to rest. Momma read a psalm from her bible as Daddy covered her up. We held hands and prayed for a minute or two, then a strange thing happened. It started to rain real gentle. There had been no clouds in the sky all day, but we felt it and looked up to the sky. Above was one dark cloud covering the sun now, blessing us with life-giving rain. We didn't leave the gravesite.

Momma finally cried. "I wanted to cry for you before but my eyes were dry as the river. Thank you, Lucinda, for sending back the rain. I know you have forgiven me for my harsh words. I didn't understand you or your uncommon gifts, for you were as natural a person as I ever met. With your help, the river will run again, our crops will grow, the well will fill, and you will be happy where you are."

Momma was right. Lucinda's curse ended. The rain returned and our little farm did okay by us for the rest of our days. I went to school when I could and one day became a wife then a mother. But I never forgot my sister, Lucinda, whose grave lies next to Momma and Daddy's now, but is the only one to sprout goldenrod every spring to feed the bees in death as she did here on earth.

ACKNOWLEDGEMENTS

First of all, thanks to the encouragement of family and friends, including: Linda Liles and Pam Greene who listened to my stories and made excellent suggestions on how to improve them; members of my Creative Writing Group who listened to them many times with a critical ear; and my friend, Eileen Proutt, who has a great eye for proofreading. And very importantly, my son, Adam Hobart, who created the cover of this book, and sorted out technical issues. I am ever so grateful!

I also want to thank Wikipedia for helping me check facts and figures online. And without the services of several search engines, I would have had to spend hours in the public library searching for who were the biggest Hollywood stars in the 1950s, what are the various kinds of pole beans, have there been cases of people changing their personalities after an organ transplant (yes, according to the National Library of Medicine), and the highlights of a cruise to the Caribbean. Donate to Wikipedia - it's an invaluable resource for writers. All clip art was free.

Davies Manor and Plantation in Bartlett, TN, is open to

the public for tours and visitors. On one such visit, I noticed the legal flier describing Mammoth, the jack donkey, framed and hanging on the wall of the house. I took a photograph and wrote the story in the persona of Logan Davies whose family owned the plantation for many years. Mammoth's antics in the story are imaginary, although not out of character for a "stubborn jackass".

Of course, this is a work of fiction. All of the characters, names, incidents, organizations, and dialogue in this book are either the products of the author's imagination or are used fictitiously.

ABOUT THE AUTHOR

Irene Becker

Having written scripts for stage plays, and hundreds of short stories over the years, Irene finally published her first book in 2022. A prodigious reader as well, she lives in a suburb of Memphis, Tennessee, with her husband and two greyhounds.

Postcards From Mom and Other Short Stories is her second book, the first being Dublin, TN, published in 2022. Dublin (a fictitious town) in East Tennessee has a long history as a railroad town, and is charming as many southern towns are. But it also has an undercurrent of corruption, mayhem, and secrets. Throw a ghost into the mix and you have a cozy that's hard to put down. A sequel is on the way - stay tuned!

Made in the USA
Columbia, SC
21 February 2023